SECOND WAVE

FIRST PRINTING: April 2008
Collecting Second Wave #1-6
10 9 8 7 6 5 4 3 2 1

PRINTED IN KOREA

ISBN-13: 978-1-934506-06-6
ISBN-10: 1-934506-06-0

SECOND WAVE

MICHAEL ALAN NELSON
WRITER

CHEE
ARTIST

ED DUKESHIRE
LETTERER

MATT WEBB
COLORIST

MARSHALL DILLON
MANAGING EDITOR

BOOM! STUDIOS

ANDREW COSBY
ROSS RICHIE
founders

MARK WAID
editor-in-chief

TOM FASSBENDER
vice president, publishing

ADAM FORTIER
vice president, new business

CHIP MOSHER
marketing & sales director

MICHAEL ALAN NELSON
associate editor

ED DUKESHIRE
designer

DANIEL VARGAS
publishing coordinator

THEY LANDED ON A TUESDAY.

BY WEDNESDAY, OUR WORLD WAS AT WAR.
AND FOR SEVEN DAYS, WE BATTLED AN ENEMY THAT WE DID NOT KNOW, DID NOT UNDERSTAND, AND COULD NOT DEFEAT.

BUT EVEN AS HUMANITY SCURRIED BEFORE THEIR DARK MACHINES, A HANDFUL OF MEN AND WOMEN RESISTED.
PEOPLE WHO STOOD AGAINST THEIR GREAT WEAPONS AND DENIED OUR ENEMIES A PAINLESS MARCH OVER OUR PLANET.
HEROES WERE BORN THAT DAY...

...I WAS NOT ONE OF THEM.
GINA, SWEETIE. WHERE'S MY PLUS-SIGN SCREWDRIVER?
YOU MEAN THE PHILLIPS HEAD, MR. GOODWRENCH? IT'S NEXT TO YOUR FOOT.

MILES, YOU SURE YOU KNOW WHAT YOU'RE DOING?

ONLY ONE WAY TO FIND OUT.

HMM... MAYBE IF I USE THE MINUS-SIGN SCREWDRIVER...

OKAY, GOOD NEWS, THE DISHWASHER WORKS. BAD NEWS, THE SINK DOESN'T.
WELL, I'D SAY CALL A PLUMBER, BUT I THINK TODAY'S A HOLIDAY.

A HOLIDAY? ARE YOU SURE?
WELL, THERE'S A PARADE GOING ON.
PRETTY BALLOONS.
YEAH. STRANGE LOOKING, THOUGH.
BUT DON'T PEOPLE USUALLY MOVE TOWARD A PARADE?
WAIT HERE.
BILL, WHAT THE HELL IS GOING ON?
ALIENS! ALIENS HAVE LANDED!

WHOA, SLOW DOWN.
THEY'RE KILLIN' EVERYBODY!
WHO IS? WHAT'S GOING--
GRAB YOUR WIFE AND RUN, MILES! RUN!

RUN FROM WHAT?
MILES? HONEY, THERE'S SOMETHING...

OH MY GOD.

THERE'S... THERE'S A FIRE ENGINE ON MY LAWN. IT'S BURNING, MILES.
I KNOW, NOW HURRY AND GET IN THE BASEMENT.
WE SHOULD PROBABLY CALL... SHOULD CALL...
CALL WHO, GINA?
THE FIRE DEPARTMENT?
C'MON, LET'S GO.
IS... IS IT ALIENS? HOW CAN IT BE ALIENS, MILES? HOW?
JUST CALM DOWN, GINA, AND GET IN THE BASEMENT.
BUT HE SAID ALIENS. I HEARD HIM SAY ALIENS!

LISTEN! I DON'T KNOW WHAT'S GOING ON. BUT YOU HAVE TO GET IN THE BASEMENT WHERE IT'S SAFE. PLEASE.
BUT...

YOU'LL BE SAFE THERE WHILE I PULL THE CAR AROUND BACK.
MILES, I DON'T WANT TO--
GINA, WE DON'T HAVE TIME TO ARGUE ABOUT THIS.

SO YOU'RE JUST GOING TO LEAVE ME?
I'M COMING RIGHT BACK.

WAIT HERE UNTIL I COME GET YOU.
BUT I WANT TO COME WITH YOU.
A FIRE TRUCK JUST LANDED IN OUR FRONT YARD, GINA. IT ISN'T SAFE.

MILES, PLEASE! DON'T LEAVE ME.
DON'T WORRY. I'LL BE RIGHT BACK.

SCREEEEEECH!

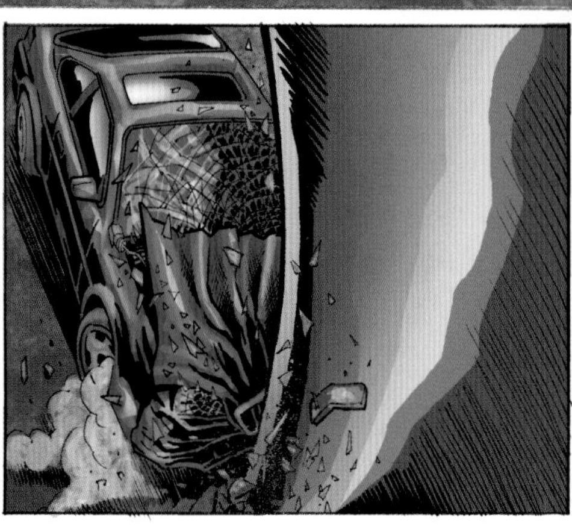

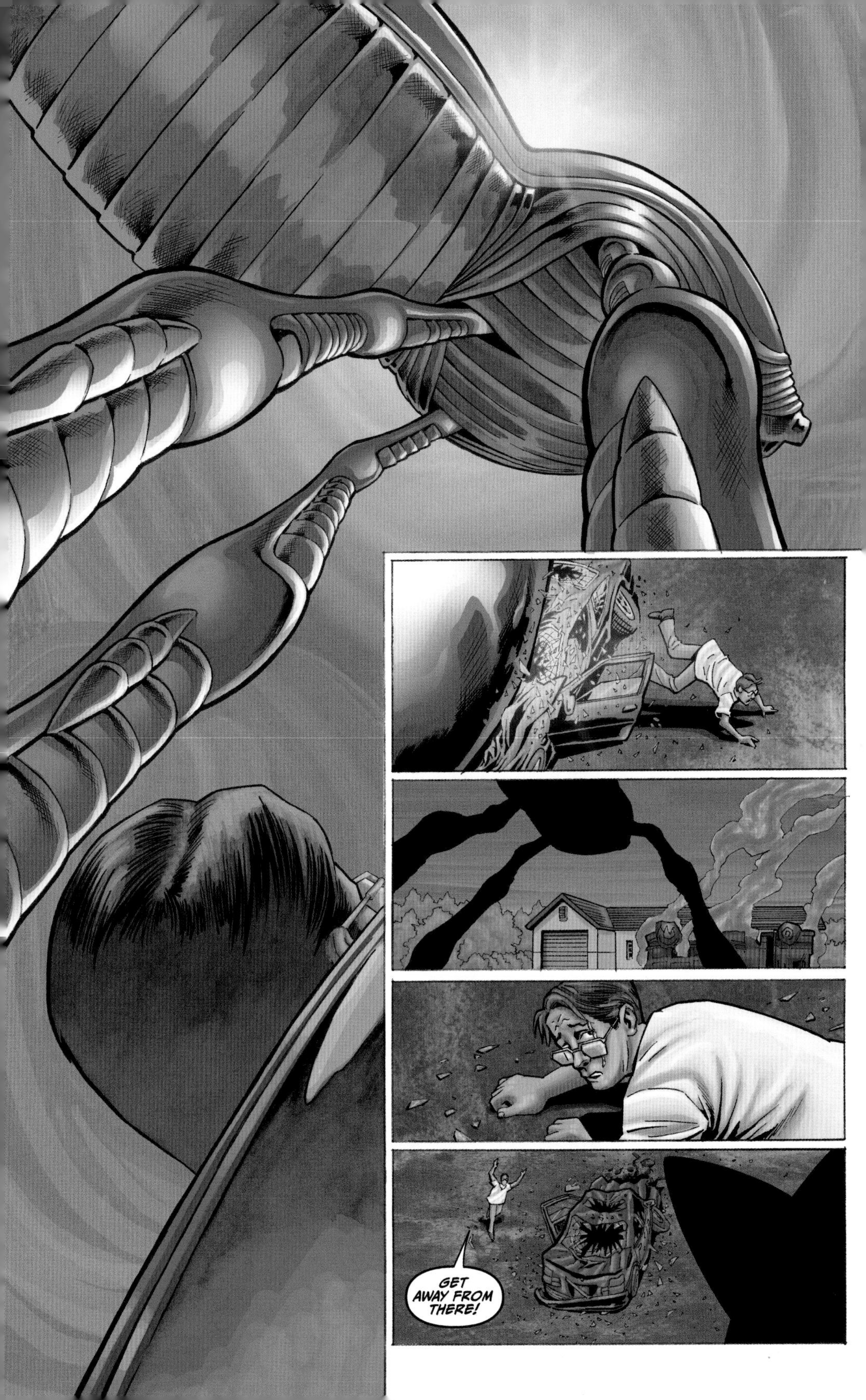
GET AWAY FROM THERE!

UUUZZZZZHHHK
KWREEETCH
CRUSH
GINA...

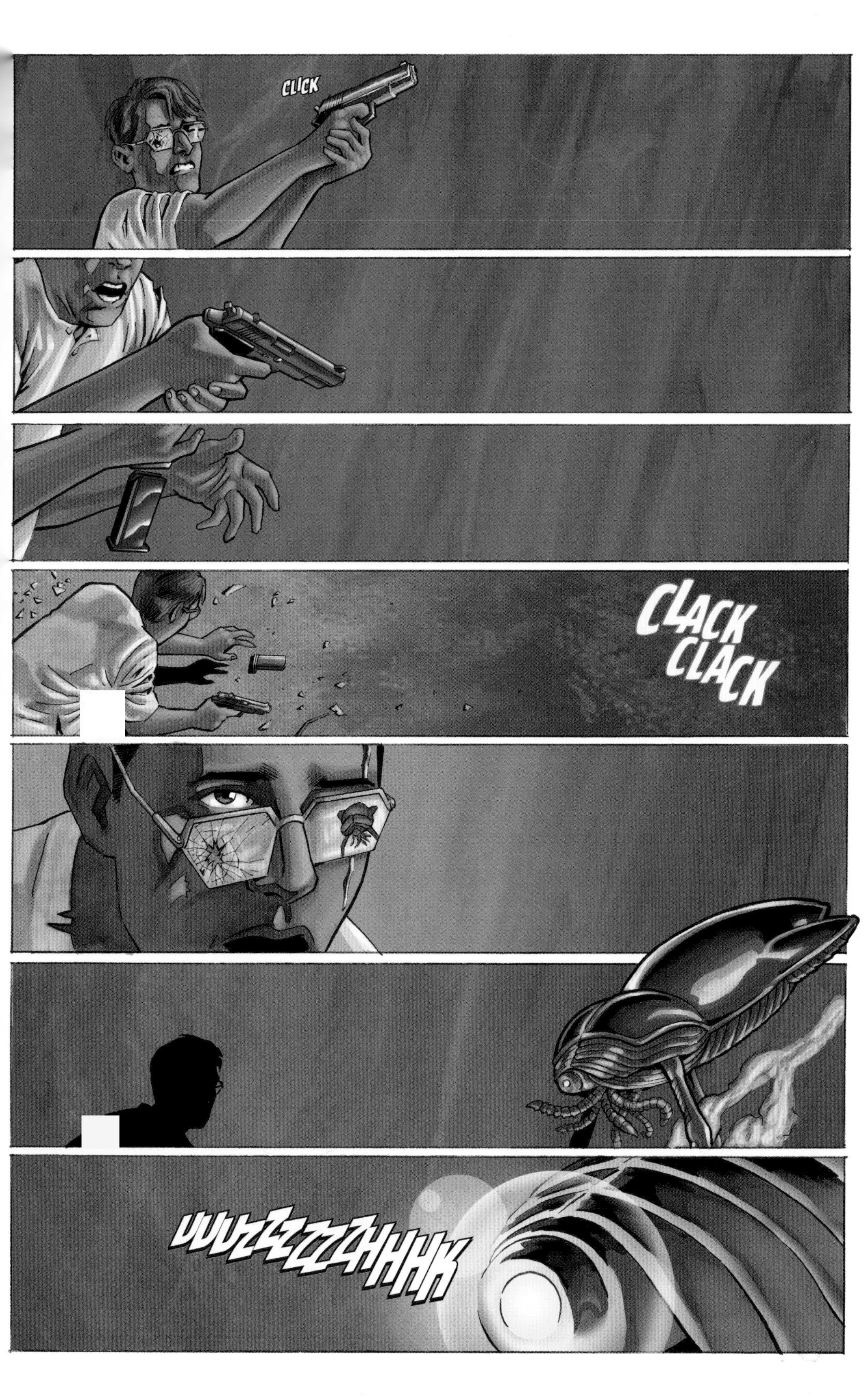
CLICK
CLACK
CLACK
UUUZZZZZZHHHK

BOOOOM!

GET BACK!
WHAPWHAP
WHAP WHAP
WHAPWHAPWHAP
GET BEHIND US!
WHAP WHAP
MY WIFE, SHE'S INSIDE. I HAVE TO HELP HER!
WHAPWHAPWHAPWHAP
TOONK TOONK
ZHIP
TOONK
UUUZZZZZZHHHK

GET THAT RPG ON ITS RIGHT FLANK!
PLEASE, I HAVE TO GET TO HER!

BIRDS ARE READY, SIR, BUT THEY NEED A VISUAL. THESE THINGS ARE EVERYWHERE.
JUST TELL THEM TO FOLLOW THE YELLOW BRICK ROAD.

KEEP YOUR HEAD DOWN.

GIVE ME COVER!

WHAP
WHAP
WHAP
TINK
CLINK
CLINK
FALL BACK! FALL BACK!
I HAVE TO GET TO MY WIFE. PLEASE!
MOVE!
INCOMING!

WHAT'S HAPPENING?
OUR GUARDIAN ANGELS ARE COMING.

AND OUR GUARDIAN ANGELS CAME.
BUT THEY DID NOT FLY ON SOARING WINGS OF FIRE AND STEEL.

INSTEAD, THEY CAME TO US ON THE DELICATE WINGS OF PESTILENCE.

AND MOTHER NATURE WHISPERED A FATAL MELODY THAT ONLY OUR ENEMIES COULD HEAR.

ELM ST.
IN THE WEEKS AFTER THE DYING, WE SWORE TO REBUILD THE WORLD.

WE WERE GIVEN A SECOND CHANCE TO LEARN FROM OUR MISTAKES.

TO UNDERSTAND OUR ENEMY.

TO INSURE THAT WE WOULD NEVER AGAIN FALL VICTIM TO THE UNEXPECTED.

IT WAS A NEW BEGINNING.

BUT I COULD NOT HELP BUT FEEL GUILTY. GUILTY FOR LEAVING HER.
GUILTY FOR FAILING.
GUILTY FOR SURVIVING.
SO I PRAYED. NOT JUST FOR FORGIVENESS, BUT FOR SOMETHING MORE.
SOMETHING MORE IMPORTANT THAN REDEMPTION, MORE PRECIOUS THAN ABSOLUTION.
AND AS I LOOKED TO THE HEAVENS, I KNEW THAT SOMEDAY MY DARK PRAYER WOULD BE ANSWERED.

I WOULD BE DELIVERED VENGEANCE.

THE SECOND WAVE LANDED ON A TUESDAY.

"HE LEAVES ME
IN THE DARK."

HE WON'T TELL ME WHAT'S BOTHERING HIM, NO MATTER HOW MANY TIMES I ASK.

"I'M HIS WIFE, HE SHOULD CONFIDE IN ME."
"BUT HE KEEPS EVERYTHING TO HIMSELF."

I'VE TRIED SCREAMING, YELLING, CRYING, BUT HE WON'T EVEN ARGUE WITH ME. OUR MARRIAGE IS FALLING APART AND IT'S LIKE...

"...IT'S LIKE HE JUST DOESN'T CARE."

GINA, IF MILES DIDN'T CARE, HE WOULDN'T BE HERE.
BUT A MARRIAGE CAN'T LAST WITHOUT COMMUNICATION.
"IF YOU WANT THIS TO WORK, MILES, YOU HAVE TO BE WILLING TO OPEN UP. TALK WITH YOUR WIFE."
I'M NOT SAYING YOU HAVE TO SHARE EVERYTHING, BUT YOUR WITHDRAWAL IS AFFECTING YOUR RELATIONSHIP WITH GINA.
"AND BELIEVE ME WHEN I SAY THIS, MILES. IF YOU CAN'T COMMUNICATE WITH YOUR WIFE..."
"...YOUR MARRIAGE WILL DIE."

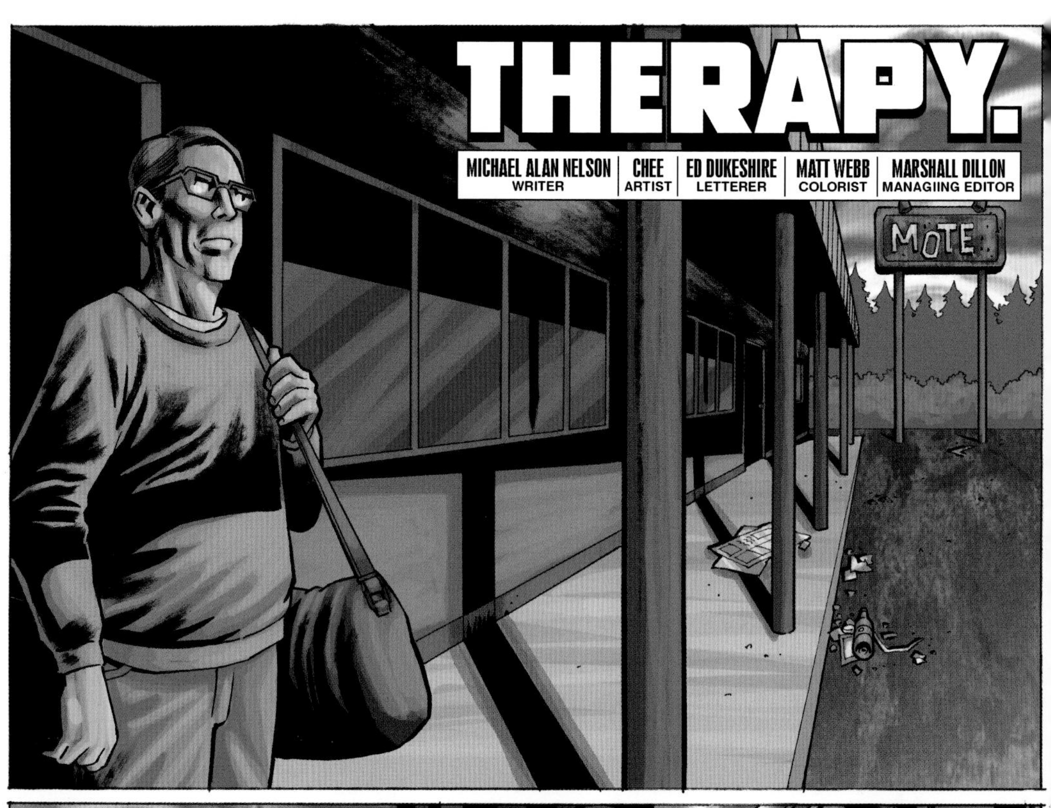
THERAPY.
MICHAEL ALAN NELSON
WRITER
CHEE
ARTIST
ED DUKESHIRE
LETTERER
MATT WEBB
COLORIST
MARSHALL DILLON
MANAGIING EDITOR
MOTE

...OUTAGES ACROSS THE MIDWEST ARE DIRECTLY RELATED TO THE SECOND WAVE OF LANDINGS.

EYEWITNESSES REPORT THAT MANY OF THE NEW PODS FALLING TO EARTH ARE NOT MOVING. THEY APPEAR TO BE DEAD ON ARRIVAL. REPEAT...
Cheevy

PACKING KINDA LIGHT, AREN'T YOU?
I'VE GOT WHAT I NEED.
...MANY OF THE RECENT LANDINGS ARE D.O.A.

CLOSED
A SECOND WAVE. MAN, YOU BELIEVE THIS? WE HAVEN'T EVEN HAD TIME TO BURY ALL THE DEAD YET.

DUKE...
THERE'LL NEVER BE ENOUGH TIME.

THE PRESIDENT HAS ORDERED EV...ONE IN ALL MAJOR METRO...TAN AREAS TO FIND U... GROUND SHELTER.
I'LL BET YOU A CAN OF CHEW AND A SIX-PACK IT'S A FALSE ALARM. JUST SOME HOLDOUTS IN ORBIT THAT GOT NOWHERE TO GO. SO THEY STICK AROUND UNTIL THEY FALL OUT OF THE SKY LIKE DEAD BIRDS.
MAYBE. BUT YOU HEARD THE GUY ON THE RADIO. THEY'RE NOT ALL D.O.A.
BESIDES, I DON'T CHEW. AND I THOUGHT YOU WERE GOING TO QUIT.
STOP
WELL, I'LL HAVE TO SOON ENOUGH. ONLY A FEW ACRES OF TOBACCO LEFT NORTH OF THE RED LINE.
BUT UNTIL THOSE ALIEN WILDFLOWERS KILL OFF ALL THE CROPS, I MIGHT AS WELL KEEP SPITTIN' AND GRINNIN'.
IF THIS REALLY IS AN ATTACK, I FIGURE ALL WE GOT TO DO IS HOLE UP FOR A WEEK OR TWO. MAYBE THEY'LL JUST DIE OFF AGAIN.
I WOULDN'T COUNT THAT.
NO? WHY NOT?
SOMETHING'S DIFFERENT.
DIFFERENT, LIKE WHAT?
I DON'T KNOW. BUT CREATURES INTELLIGENT ENOUGH TO TRAVEL THE STARS CAN'T BE SO STUPID TO THINK THAT REPEATING THE SAME ACTIONS OVER AND OVER AGAIN WILL PRODUCE DIFFERENT RESULTS. THAT'S CLINICALLY INSANE.
SOMETHING'S HAD TO HAVE CHANGED.
WELL I'M ALL FOR PUTTING THEM IN THE CRAZY CAMP. PARATROOPING DEAD SOLDIERS INTO ENEMY TERRITORY DON'T SOUND LIKE BRILLIANT MILITARY STRATEGY TO ME.
YEAH, BUT THAT'S WHAT BOTHERS ME ABOUT THE WHOLE THING.
...IPODS ARE MOVING ...OUGH ALL ...REAS UNH...DERED.
WHO SAYS THEY'RE DEAD?

WELL, IF THEY'RE NOT DOING ANYTHING, THE ALIENS INSIDE ARE EITHER DEAD OR THEIR TRIPODS ARE BROKEN.
EITHER WAY SUITS ME JUST FINE.
I DON'T KNOW, DUKE. THEY HAVE TO DO SOMETHING. THERE HAS TO BE A REASON.
...PEOPLE ARE...NING IN PANI...
HELL IF I KNOW WHAT IT IS. YOU ASK ME, I THINK YOU GIVE THEM TOO MUCH CREDIT. YEAH YEAH, THEY GOT THE WHOLE SPACE TRAVEL THING GOING ON, BUT C'MON! THEY HAVEN'T EVEN DISCOVERED THE WHEEL.
...HE SKY... BURNING...
NOT TOO BRIGHT IN MY BOOK.
DUKE!
OH S--
SCREEEEEECH!

THUUDDD!
COME ON! MOVE, YOU CRAPTACULAR PIECE OF JUNK!

WHAT THE HELL ARE YOU DOING?
WE'LL ROCK IT OUT. JUST KEEP IT IN REVERSE!

ERRRRAAAYAAAAHHHHH!

OKAY, LET'S GO! AND NEXT TIME, *YOU* HAVE TO--
WAIT.

IT'S NOT DOING ANYTHING.

DAMMIT DUKE, THE REASON WE'RE BOTH STILL ALIVE IS BECAUSE WE DON'T DO STUPID THINGS LIKE STAND AROUND *WAITING* FOR IT TO DO SOMETHING, NOW LET'S GO!

BLAM!

SEE? TOLD YA. NOTHING BUT A DEAD BIRD.

WHOOOOSSHH

VVVZZZZZZHHHK
DRIVE!

VVVZZZZZZHHHK
IS IT FOLLOWING US?
YOU SHOT IT, DUKE! OF COURSE IT'S FOLLOWING US!

THERE, THERE! TAKE THAT EXIT ONTO THE HIGHWAY. HURRY!
BOOOOM!
EXIT FASTER! EXIT FASTER!
WILL YOU STOP SIDE-SEAT DRIVING! WHERE THE HELL'RE WE GOING ANYWAY?
THE COUNTRY. IF WE MAKE IT, WE SHOULD BE SAFE FOR A WHILE.
VVVZZZ
IF WE MAKE IT.
GET DOWN!
ZZZHHHHK

HRRRAAAAHH!!!!

DUKE! ARE YOU ALL RIGHT?

MY TRUCK.

LOOK WHAT THAT THREE-LEGGED BASTARD DID TO MY TRUCK!

MILES, WHAT ARE YOU DOING?

RUNNING!

"THOUGHT YOU
COULD HIDE FROM
ME, DIDN'T YOU?"

NEXT TIME, TRY A BAR OUTSIDE OF TOWN.
GO AWAY, DUKE.
"NOT A CHANCE. YOU AND I ARE GOING TO HAVE A LITTLE TALK."
SORRY, BUT I DON'T FEEL LIKE TALKING.
GOOD, 'CAUSE I DON'T FEEL LIKE LISTENING.
BUT I AM GOING TO SAY MY PIECE AND YOU'RE GOING TO PAY ATTENTION.
"YOUR WORLD IS FALLING APART, MAN."
"YOU'RE DRINKING YOURSELF TO DEATH WHILE YOUR WIFE IS HOME ALONE, WORRIED SICK ABOUT YOU."

"YOU DON'T WANT TO TALK TO ME, FINE. I AIN'T INTO ALL THAT TOUCHY-FEELY CRAP ANYWAY. BUT YOU BETTER GET HELP."
WE'VE BEEN BEST FRIENDS SINCE WE WERE PUPS, MILES. I'D DO ANYTHING FOR YOU, YOU KNOW THAT.

"BUT I AIN'T WATCHING YOU DO THIS TO YOURSELF."
"OR TO GINA."

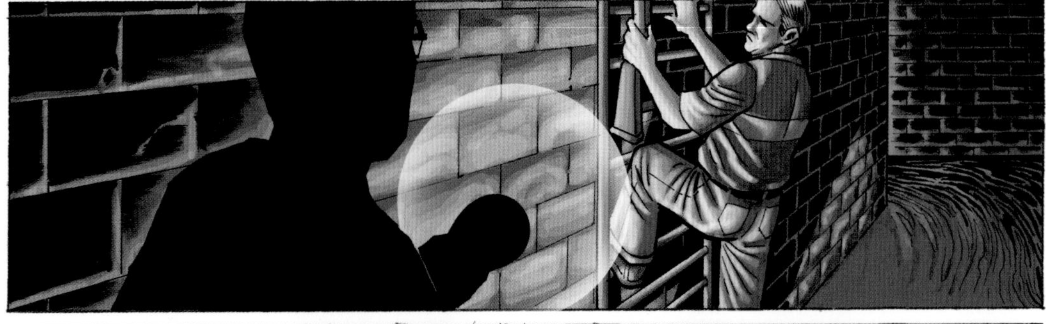

"YOU KEEP THIS UP, ONE DAY YOU'RE GOING TO TURN AROUND..."

"...AND THERE'LL BE NOBODY THERE."

IT'S OKAY. FRIENDLIES HERE.

DIDN'T MEAN TO FRIGHTEN ANYONE.
IT'S OKAY. I GUESS WE'RE JUST A LITTLE SCARED OF THE LIGHT.

THEY STILL UP THERE?
YEAH. BUT NOT AS MANY AS AN HOUR AGO.
DO YOU HAVE ANY FOOD?

NOT MUCH, BUT YOU'RE WELCOME TO IT.
IT'S ONLY BEEN A FEW HOURS, BUT WE'RE STARVING.

DUKE?
NAH. TOO TIRED TO EAT.

HOW MANY PEOPLE YOU HAVE WITH YOU?
JUST WHAT YOU SEE HERE. I'M BUTCH. THIS HERE'S JANE.
MMPHH... MMHI...

AND THAT'S MY DAUGHTER, CORA.
STEP-DAUGHTER.
YES, STEP-DAUGHTER.

I'M MILES, AND THIS IS DUKE.
YEAH.
WELL, I'D SAY IT WAS NICE TO MEET YOU, BUT...

HOW LONG UNTIL THEY DIE OFF AGAIN DO YOU THINK?
NOT SURE. BUT WE DEFINITELY DON'T HAVE ENOUGH FOOD AND WATER TO WAIT THEM OUT.

TELL 'EM ABOUT YOUR THEORY.
SHUT UP.

WE HAD FOOD IN OUR TRUCK BEFORE IT WAS...DESTROYED. IT MIGHT STILL BE GOOD.
WE CAN CHECK FIRST THING IN THE MORNING. IF THEY'VE MOVED ON, WE CAN GET THE FOOD. IT'S NOT FAR FROM HERE.

UNTIL THEN, WE SHOULD PROBABLY TRY AND GET SOME SLEEP WHILE WE CAN.
NEED TO SET UP A WATCH. FIGURE WE'LL DIVIDE IT THREE WAYS BETWEEN THE MEN.
GOOD IDEA. SINCE YOU BROUGHT THE FOOD, I'LL TAKE MIDDLE WATCH. LEAST I CAN DO.
YOU GET SOME SLEEP, BROTHER.
I THOUGHT YOU SAID YOU WERE TOO TIRED TO EAT.
I DID. I'M ALSO TOO TIRED TO SLEEP. NOW GO. I'LL WAKE YOU UP IF THERE'S TROUBLE.
"DON'T WORRY, MILES. THESE PRIVATE SESSIONS ARE CONFIDENTIAL."
NOTHING YOU SAY HERE WILL BE MENTIONED DURING YOUR SESSIONS WITH GINA.
SO TELL ME WHAT'S BEEN BOTHERING YOU.
"..."
">SIGH< I'VE BEEN HAVING..."
"...DREAMS."

"IT'S DARK. I'M ALONE, NAKED. CAN'T BREATHE. THERE'S SOMETHING AROUND MY FACE. MY NECK."

"THE MONSTERS."

I'M...

...NOT...

...CRAZY.
CLICK

NO ONE IS SAYING YOU ARE, MILES...

REMEDY.
...BUT THESE WILL HELP.
HELP WHAT?
WRITTEN BY
MICHAEL ALAN NELSON
DRAWN BY CHEE
COLORS BY
MATT WEBB
LETTERS BY
ED DUKESHIRE
COVER BY SUNDER RAJ
MANAGING EDITING BY
MARSHALL DILLON
HELP THE MONSTERS GO AWAY.

YOU OKAY, HOSS?
NO, NOT BY A LONG SHOT.
IT WAS THEM, DUKE. THEY DID THIS TO ME.
THEY'RE THE ONES THAT CAME FOR ME IN THE NIGHT. ABDUCTED ME. MADE ME THINK I WAS GOING CRAZY, IMAGINING THINGS.
THEY'RE THE REASON MY MARRIAGE FELL APART.
I THOUGHT IT WAS 'CAUSE YOU COULDN'T GET IT UP ANYMORE.

JANE, I'M SORRY, BUT WE HAVE TO GO. MORE WILL COME.
SOON.
PLEASE, WE HAVE TO--
DON'T YOU TOUCH ME!
DON'T YOU EVER TOUCH ME.
COME ON, CORA.
GO ON AHEAD. I THINK IT'D BE BEST IF I LAG BEHIND FOR BIT.
YOU'RE THE BOSS, HOSS. BUT DON'T LAG FOR TOO LONG.
I'LL BE RIGHT BEHIND YOU, NOW GO.

WHAT'S GOING ON? WHY'D YOU STOP?
END OF THE LINE.
GREAT.
MAYBE WE SHOULD DOUBLE BACK.
I DON'T WANT TO GO BACK THERE.
DOESN'T LOOK LIKE WE HAVE A CHOICE. THE WATER'S TOO DEEP FOR US TO--
...THHMMMMMFFFZZZZZZ...
THEY'RE COMING.
KILL THE LIGHT.

KIND OF LIKE CUSTER'S LAST STAND.
THE ALAMO.
OR THE HOUSECARLS OF KING GODWINSON.
THERMOPYLAE.

SNOB.
THOSE WHO DON'T STUDY HISTORY ARE DOOMED TO--
SPLASH!

MILES?

WHERE'D HE GO?
I DON'T KNOW. MILES? MILES!
MOM, I THINK THEY'RE COMING.

DAMMIT.
DAMMIT, WHERE THE HELL IS HE?

RIGHT HERE. I SLIPPED, BUT THINK I FOUND A WAY UNDER THE CAVE-IN.
CAN YOU LADIES SWIM?

IN SEWER WATER? UGHH...
HURRY. IT'S NOT FAR.

HEY, DON'T GO ALL HAMLET ON ME. LET'S LIVE TO FIGHT ANOTHER DAY, OKAY?

NOW WHO'S THE SNOB?
WELL I AIN'T JUST A PRETTY FACE. C'MON.

I'M TIRED. CAN WE STOP NOW?
NOT YET. WE'RE JUST OUTSIDE THE CITY LIMITS. IT SHOULD BE SAFE TO LEAVE THE SEWERS FROM HERE.
HOW ARE WE GOING TO GET OUT? NOT TOO MANY MANHOLE COVERS OUT IN THE STICKS.

THIS DRAINAGE PIPE SHOULD WORK. IT'LL BE TIGHT, BUT IT SHOULD LEAD US OUT.

I DON'T WANT TO GO IN THERE. I CAN'T.
YES YOU CAN. JUST THINK OF THE WIDE, OPEN SKY AND YOU'LL BE FINE.

I'LL GO FIRST. STAY CLOSE BEHIND ME.

I DON'T KNOW IF I CAN DO THIS.
CORA, IF A HOSS LIKE ME CAN FIT, SO CAN YOU.
"I NEED AIR."
MOM, I...I CAN'T BREATHE. IT'S TOO TIGHT.
DON'T THINK ABOUT IT.
"IT FEELS LIKE I'M SUFFOCATING."
I HAVE TO GET OUT OF HERE.
CALM DOWN. WE'RE ALMOST--
NO! I CAN'T TAKE IT ANY MORE. I... PLEASE HURRY... OH GOD I CAN'T...
"...I CAN'T BREATHE!"
IT'S OKAY, CORA. WE MADE IT. CAN YOU HOLD ON JUST A FEW MORE SECONDS WHILE I SEE IF IT'S SAFE?
...YES.
GOOD.

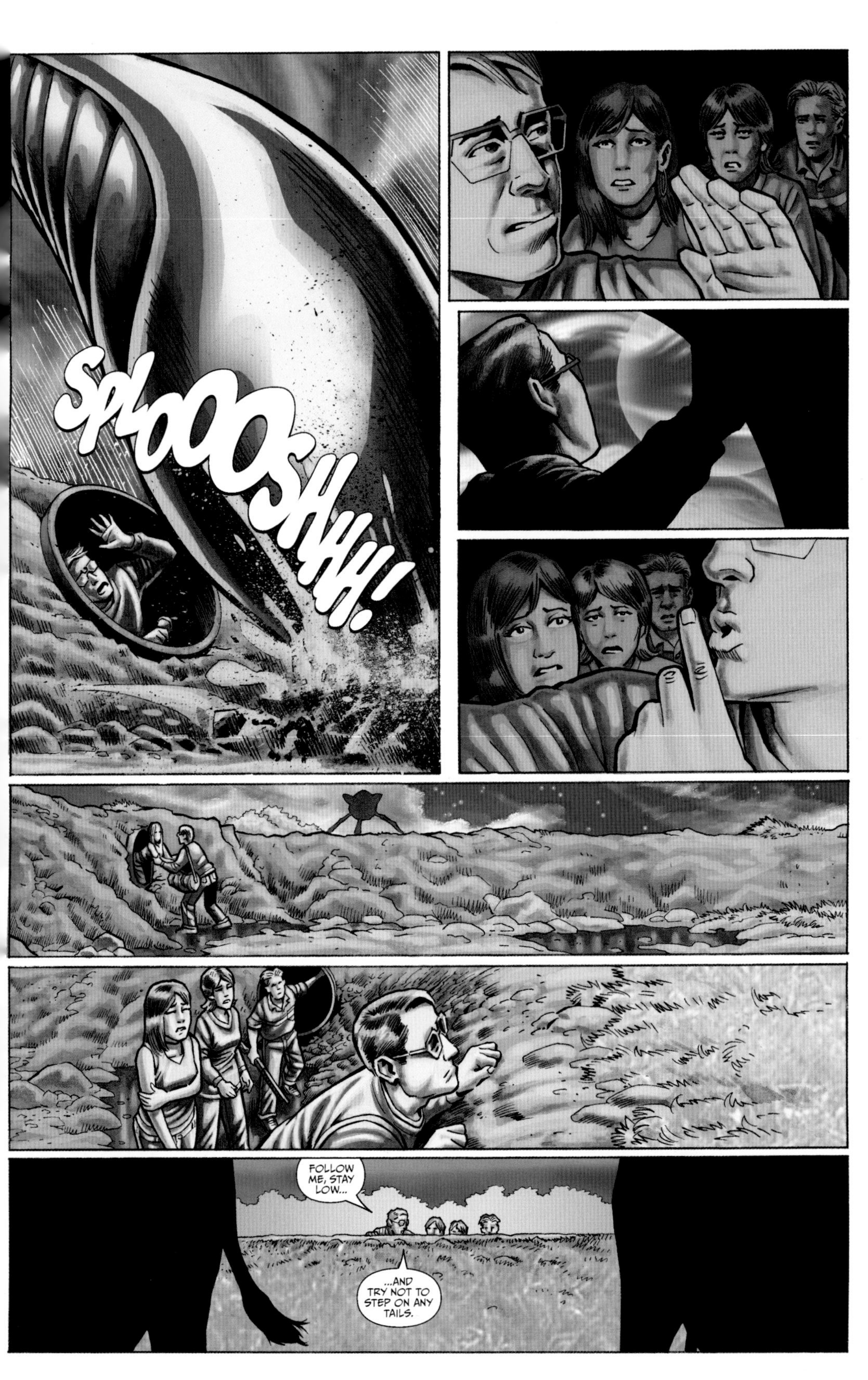
SPLOOOSHHH!
FOLLOW ME, STAY LOW...
...AND TRY NOT TO STEP ON ANY TAILS.

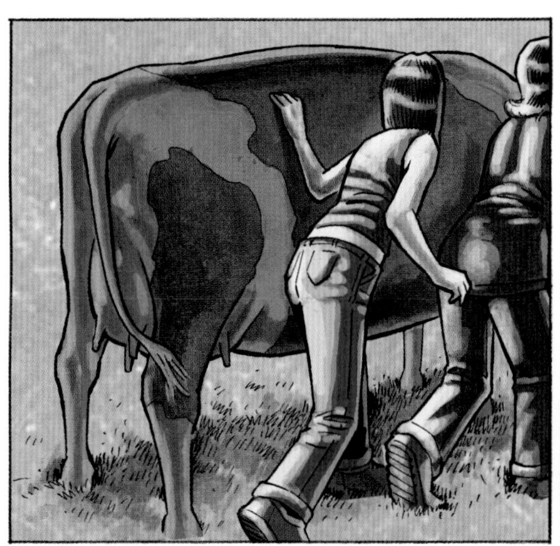

MOOOO...
AHH!

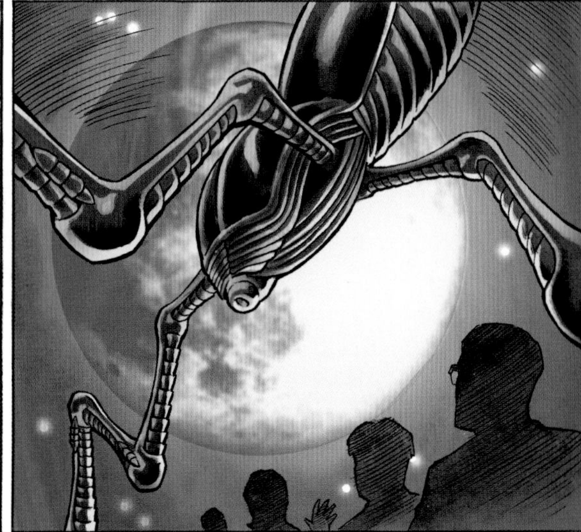

RUN!

BLAM!

WHAT THE HELL ARE YOU DOING?!?!
DISTRACTING THEM!
HAVE YOU LOST YOUR MIND? YOU'RE GONNA GET US ALL--

ZZZHHHTTTT

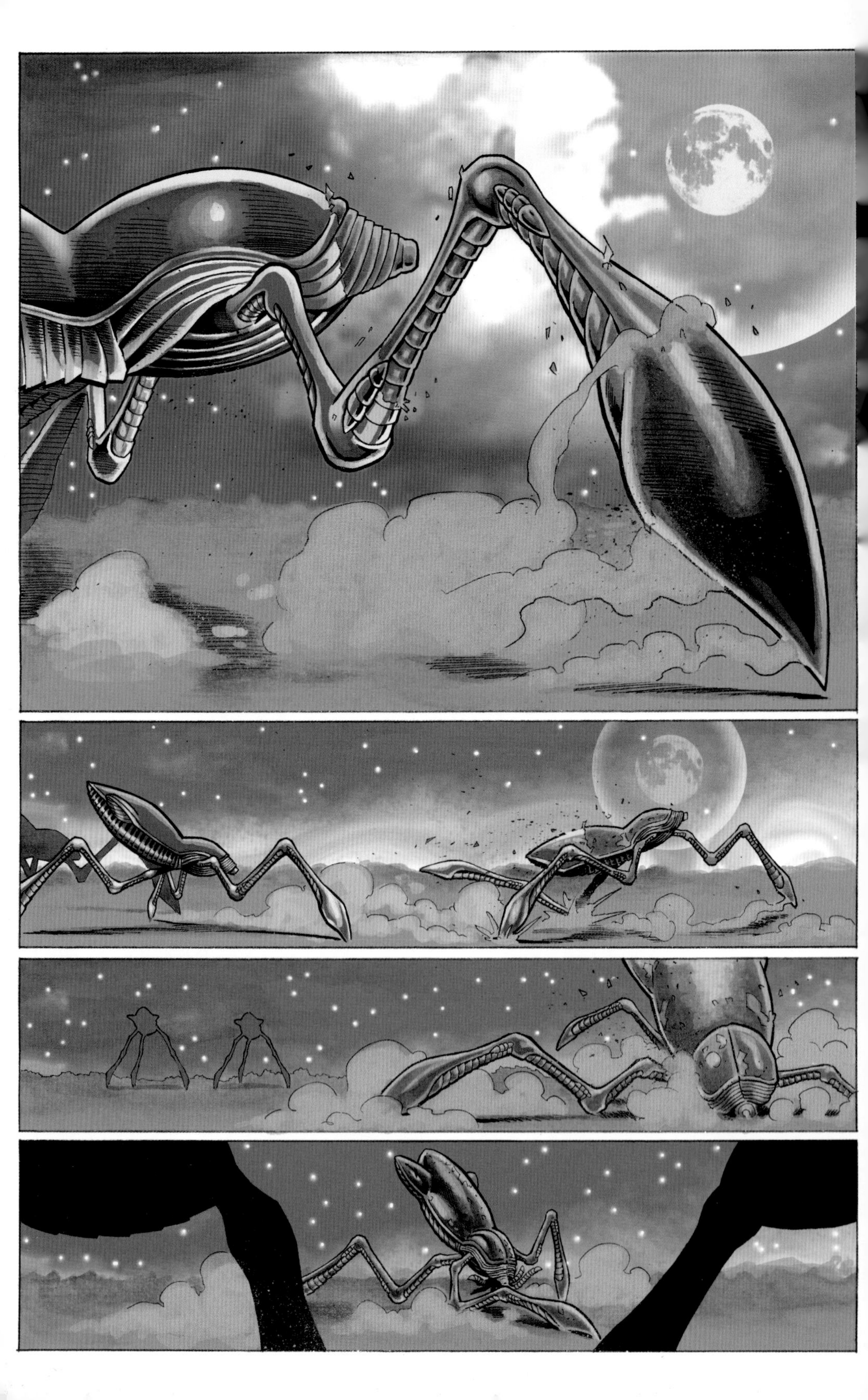

WHAT THE HELL? DID...DID THEY JUST FRY ONE OF THEIR OWN?
YEAH. LOOKED LIKE IT LOST ALL ITS COLOR...THEN THEY JUST *SHOT* IT.
I TOLD YOU THEY WERE COMPLETELY BUGNUTS.
MAYBE.
AT LEAST THEY'RE NOT FOLLOWING US.

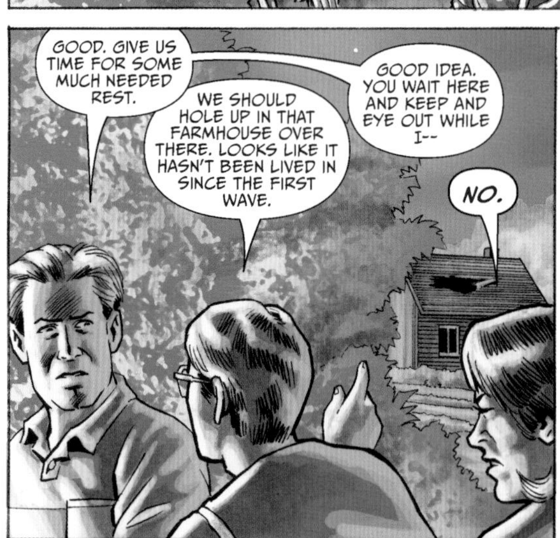
GOOD. GIVE US TIME FOR SOME MUCH NEEDED REST.
WE SHOULD HOLE UP IN THAT FARMHOUSE OVER THERE. LOOKS LIKE IT HASN'T BEEN LIVED IN SINCE THE FIRST WAVE.
GOOD IDEA. YOU WAIT HERE AND KEEP AND EYE OUT WHILE I--
NO.

HE'S NOT VERY GOOD AT KEEPING WATCH. DUKE, YOU STAY. MAKE HIM GO.
MOM, IT'S NOT HIS FAULT BUTCH DIED.
THAT'S RIGHT. IF IT WASN'T FOR MILES--
IT'S OKAY, DUKE. I'LL GO.

IF I'M NOT BACK IN TEN MINUTES...
I'LL BE COMING IN RIGHT AFTER YOU, HOSS. DON'T EVEN TRY TO ARGUE DIFFERENT. NOW GO.

OH, NO.
I THINK MILES MIGHT BE IN TROUBLE.
WHY, WHAT IS IT?

SOMEONE'S HOME.

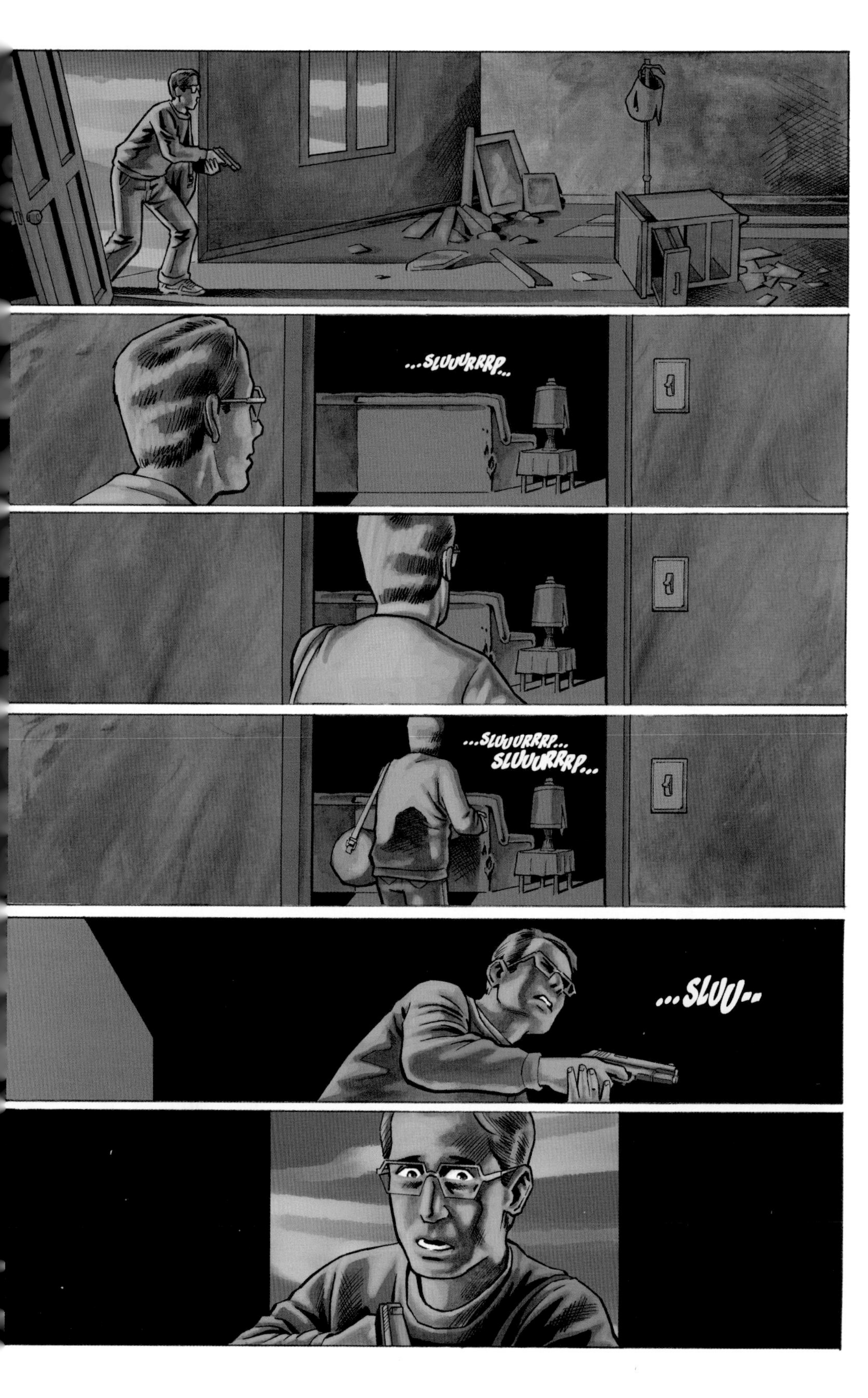
...SLUUURRRP...
...SLUUURRRP...
SLUUURRRP...
...SLUU-.

...
PEOP

OH.
HELLO.

CLICK

GOODBYE.

TOSS THE GUN. AND MAN, YOU SO MUCH AS TWITCH WRONG...
NO TWITCHING, GOT IT.
DESPERATION
MICHAEL ALAN NELSON WRITER
CHEE ARTIST
MATT WEBB COLORIST
ED DUKESHIRE LETTERER
SUNDER RAJ COVER

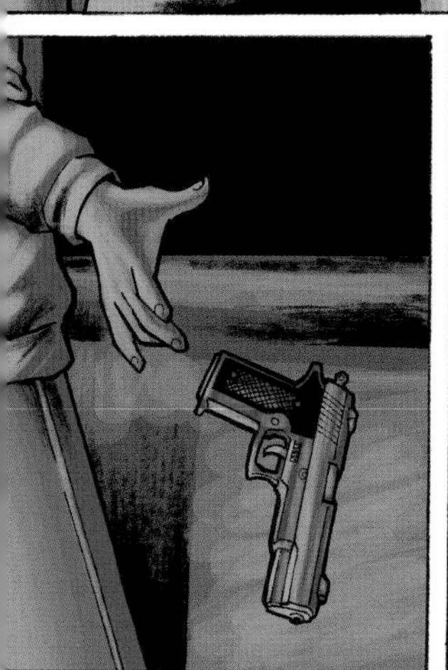

DAD?
GO IN THE OTHER ROOM, BABY. YOU DON'T NEED TO SEE THIS.
BUT DAD--
NOW, RONNI.

I...I THINK THERE'S BEEN A MISTAKE.
DAMN RIGHT. YOU POINTED A GUN AT MY LITTLE GIRL.

I DIDN'T KNOW IT WAS A GIRL.
TOO BAD FOR YOU.
DROP IT!

PUT IT DOWN, SLOWLY.

AIN'T HAPPENING, MAN. NO ONE THREATENS MY GIRL AND WALKS.
DAD, PLEASE.
STAY BACK, RONNI.
OKAY, LET'S ALL CALM DOWN HERE. THIS IS JUST A MISUNDERSTANDING.

NO MISUNDERSTANDING A GUN IN MY DAUGHTER'S FACE.

WELL YOU'RE STARING AT THE BUSINESS END OF A WHOLE *WORLD* OF UNDERSTANDING NOW.
LET HIM GO.

PLEASE. DUKE, IT'S OKAY. JANE, YOU TOO. JUST PUT THE GUN DOWN. YOU DON'T REALLY WANT TO HURT HIM.

I'M NOT AIMING IT AT ***HIM.***

IT SHOULD HAVE BEEN YOU, MILES. NOT BUTCH. IT SHOULD HAVE KILLED YOU.

JANE, DON'T CREATE A PROBLEM FOR YOURSELF.
IT ATE HIM. THAT THING *ATE* MY HUSBAND.
MOM! WHAT ARE YOU DOING?

WHAT'S SHE TALKING ABOUT?
HER HUSBAND WAS KILLED BY AN ALIEN. SUCKED DRY. THAT'S WHAT I THOUGHT I HEARD WHEN I CAME IN. WHY I POINTED A GUN AT YOUR DAUGHTER.

IT SHOULD HAVE BEEN YOU.
JANE, PLEASE DON'T MAKE ME KILL YOU IN FRONT OF YOUR DAUGHTER. JUST GIVE ME THE GUN.

TAKE IT.

LOOK. NO ONE WANTS TO HURT YOUR GIRL. WE'RE RUNNIN', SAME AS YOU. BUT YOU SHOOT MY FRIEND, YOU'RE GETTING' A FACE FULL OF BUCKSHOT.

PLEASE DAD, LET HIM GO.

I JUST WANT TO MAKE SURE YOU'RE SAFE, BABY.

YOU ALL RIGHT?
KIND OF SHAKY, BUT I'LL BE FINE. THAT WAS A FAST TEN MINUTES.
WE THOUGHT THERE MIGHT BE SOMEBODY IN THE HOUSE.

SOMEBODY... *SQUIDIER*.

THERE'S A TRIPOD STICKING OUT OF THE SIDE OF THE HOUSE.

LEFTOVER FROM THE DYING. I CHECKED IT OUT WHEN WE GOT HERE.
SO I CAN GO LOOK AT IT NOW?

ABSOLUTELY NOT.
BUT...
NO. WE'RE LEAVING.

I'M THINKING WE SHOULD BE DOIN' THE SAME.
YEAH, SOON. I SHOULD PROBABLY GO CHECK ON JANE AND CORA.

MAYBE YOU SHOULD WAIT HERE. SEE IF YOU CAN GO THE NEXT FIVE MINUTES WITHOUT SOMEONE TRYING TO PUT A BULLET IN YOUR HEAD.

HOW'S SHE DOING?
SHE'S PRETTY FREAKED OUT.
YEAH.
NO HARD FEELINGS, I HOPE.

NAH. SOMETIMES I WISH I COULD POINT A GUN AT HER.

WELL, SHE'S IN A TOUGH SPOT. IT'S NOT EASY LOSING SOMEBODY YOU CARE ABOUT.
YEAH? YOU EVER LOSE ANYBODY?

WE'VE ALL LOST SOMEBODY.

MY DAD SAYS THEY GOT SICK.

THAT'S CERTAINLY ONE THEORY.
COULD WE CATCH IT TOO?
I DON'T KNOW. I GUESS IT DEPENDS IF WE MADE THEM SICK OR IF THEY WERE ALREADY SICK WHEN THEY GOT HERE.

I HOPE NOT. IT'S NO FUN BEING SICK.

SO WHY'D THEY COME BACK?
I DON'T KNOW. BUT THE FACT THAT THEY DID MAKES ME WONDER ABOUT THE WHOLE "THEY GOT SICK" THEORY.
GUESS WE'LL FIND OUT EVENTUALLY.

RONNI, I THOUGHT I TOLD YOU NOT TO GO NEAR THAT THING.
BUT I'VE NEVER SEEN ONE UP CLOSE. TOUCH IT. IT FEELS LIKE A CAT'S TONGUE.

I DON'T CARE. I DON'T WANT YOU ANYWHERE NEAR THESE THINGS, UNDERSTAND?
BUT DAD, I JUST WANTED TO...

...JUST WANTED...
LOOK...

RONNI!

BABY, WAKE UP, COME ON STAY WITH ME. RONNI STAY WITH ME.
WHAT HAPPENED?
WATER, I NEED WATER. COME ON BABY, TALK TO ME.

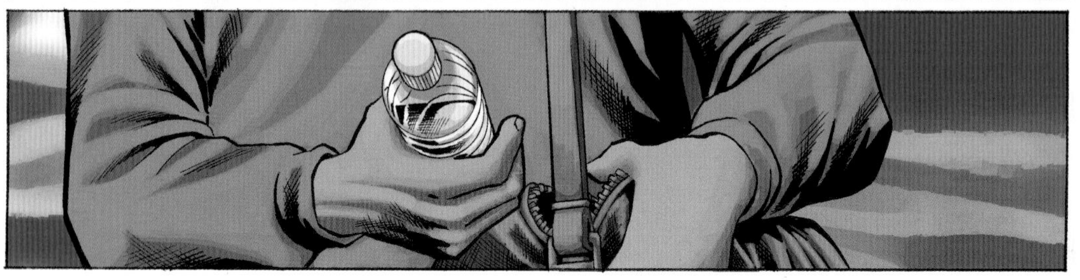

SMALL SIPS, BABY. SMALL SIPS. GOOD GIRL.
IS SHE OKAY?
SHE'S DIABETIC. HASN'T HAD ANY INSULIN FOR A WHILE. HER BLOOD SUGAR'S TOO HIGH AND SHE GETS DIZZY PRETTY EASY.
I'M FINE, DAD. JUST TIRED IS ALL.

AFTER THE DYING, WE TRIED TO FIND A HOSPITAL IN THE CITY, BUT THERE WEREN'T ANY LEFT.
I LOOKED EVERYWHERE FOR INSULIN. CLINICS, RETIREMENT HOMES, DRUG STORES. BUT ALL THE ONES THAT WEREN'T WIPED OUT WERE EMPTY.

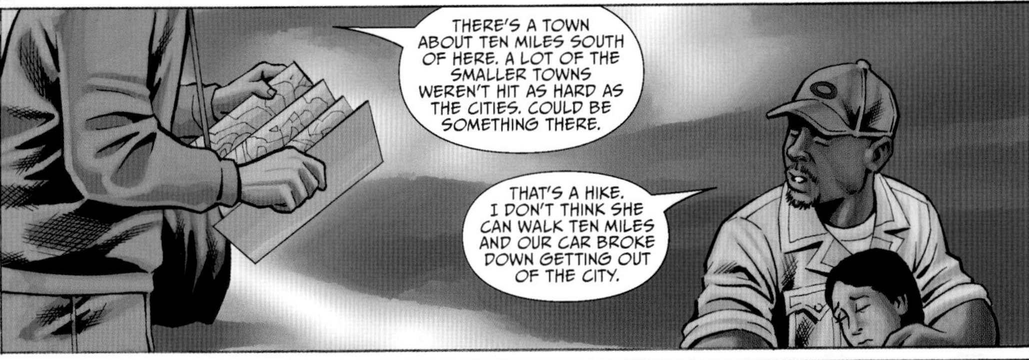
THERE'S A TOWN ABOUT TEN MILES SOUTH OF HERE. A LOT OF THE SMALLER TOWNS WEREN'T HIT AS HARD AS THE CITIES. COULD BE SOMETHING THERE.
THAT'S A HIKE. I DON'T THINK SHE CAN WALK TEN MILES AND OUR CAR BROKE DOWN GETTING OUT OF THE CITY.

BUT I'LL THINK OF SOMETHING. I ALWAYS TAKE CARE OF MY BABY.

DUKE, I NEED YOU FOR A SECOND.
WHAT EXACTLY ARE WE LOOKING FOR?
THAT.
THINK IT RUNS?
IF IT'S GOT GAS AND A KEY IN THE IGNITION, I'D SAY FIFTY FIFTY.
THAT'S BETTER ODDS THAN WE'VE SEEN IN A WHILE.
DON'T YOU THINK WE SHOULD FIND SOMETHING... I DON'T KNOW. SMALLER?
WOULDN'T WORK. NOT WITH ALL OF US.
ALL OF US, HUH? YOU SURE THAT'S A GOOD IDEA?
YEAH. WHY NOT?
WELL, THAT GIRL'S DAD DID HAVE A GUN TO YOUR HEAD NOT MORE THAN TEN MINUTES AGO.

HE WAS JUST SCARED. HE DIDN'T KNOW.
MAYBE. BUT WHAT ABOUT JANE? THAT WOMAN HATES YOU. SOONER OR LATER SHE'S GOING TO TRY AND KILL YOU AGAIN.
SO YOU THINK WE SHOULD LEAVE HER?
WELL... YEAH.

WHAT IF IT WAS GINA?
WELL IT'S NOT. LOOK, THE WORLD IS FILLED WITH WIDOWS NOW, AND YOU CAN'T SAVE THEM ALL. I UNDERSTAND WHAT YOU'RE TRYING TO DO, MILES. BUT SHE'S NOT YOUR WIFE.

NO, BUT SHE WAS ***SOMEONE'S*** WIFE.
WE CAN'T LEAVE HER, DUKE. IT WOULDN'T BE RIGHT.

YOU'RE THE BOSS, HOSS. I GOT YOUR BACK EITHER WAY. BUT DON'T COME CRYIN' TO ME IF ONE OF THOSE TWO SHOOTS YOU.

CORA, WE'RE GOING TO BE LEAVING SOON. IF YOU AND YOUR MOM DON'T WANT TO COME, I'LL UNDERSTAND. BUT IF SO, MEET US AROUND BACK.

I THINK WE MAY HAVE FOUND SOMETHING. YOU READY?
WHERE'RE WE GOING?
FOR A HAYRIDE.

SO, WHERE WE HEADED?
EDDINGTON. SMALL TOWN NOT FAR FROM HERE.
WHAT'S IN EDDINGTON?
WITH ANY LUCK, A HOSPITAL. THAT RONNI GIRL'S PRETTY SICK.
SICK. UH HUH.
YOU KNOW, IF THIS BECOMES A HABIT WITH YOU, I'M GOING TO START MAKING YOU WEAR A CAPE.
HEY JAMES, WE SHOULD BE THERE IN A FEW HOURS.
WELL, LET'S HOPE WE GET THERE BEFORE THEY NOTICE US.

WE'RE SAFE FOR NOW. THREE OF THEM WERE CHASING US THIS MORNING. BUT WHEN ONE CROSSED THE RIVER TO FOLLOW US, THE OTHER TWO KILLED IT. THEY HAVEN'T COME AFTER US SINCE.

MAYBE THEY CAN'T SWIM.
COULD BE. WOULDN'T MAKE MUCH SENSE THOUGH.
YEAH, WELL NOTHING IN THIS WORLD MAKES SENSE.
NOT ANYMORE.

WELCOME
TO
REDDINGTON

r3d h34dz
r00l
GESUNDHEIT

HOLD UP FOLKS. YOU CAN'T TAKE THAT INTO TOWN.

THERE'S TOO MUCH DEBRIS IN THE ROAD. YOU'LL NEVER GET THAT THROUGH.
YOU GOT A HOSPITAL HERE?
NO, BUT I THINK A LOCAL DOC'S GOT AN OFFICE DOWN-TOWN. BUT GOOD LUCK GETTING THERE.
THEY'VE LANDED HERE ALREADY?
NO, NOT YET. BUT THE LOCALS ARE HAVING SOME...ISSUES AT THE MOMENT. WHEN THE SQUIDS STARTED LANDING AGAIN, THE ONLY GROCER IN TOWN CLOSED UP SHOP AND KEPT ALL THE FOOD FOR HIMSELF. GOT HIS STORE LOCKED DOWN LIKE FORT KNOX.
THIS MORNING THEY BURNED HIM OUT.
TOOK THEM A COUPLE MINUTES TO REALIZE THE FOOD WAS BURNING TOO.
WHY DIDN'T YOU GUYS TRY TO STOP IT?
ARE YOU KIDDING? IT'S MOB RULE IN THERE. AND THERE'S JUST THE THREE OF US.
WELL, WHAT ABOUT THE COPS? ISN'T THERE A SHERIFF IN TOWN?
YEAH, THEY GOT ONE.
WHO DO YOU THINK STARTED THE FIRE?

RONNI, YOU WAIT HERE WITH THE SOLDIERS.
DAD, NO. DON'T LEAVE ME. LET ME COME WITH YOU.
NO, SWEETIE. IT'S NOT SAFE FOR YOU IN THERE. YOU STAY HERE.

I THINK YOU SHOULD LISTEN TO HER, MAN. THEY AIN'T IN A FRIENDLY MOOD. AND SOME OF THESE PEOPLE PROBABLY WON'T LIKE THE IDEA OF, UH...*CITY FOLK* COMING THROUGH THEIR TOWN.
YEAH, AND WHAT EXACTLY IS THAT SUPPOSED TO MEAN?
HEY, I'M JUST SAYING.

'FRAID THE MAN'S RIGHT, JAMES. IT'S NOT SAFE.
I DON'T CARE ABOUT "SAFE." I'M NOT GONNA STAND HERE AND WATCH MY LITTLE GIRL WASTE AWAY BECAUSE A BUNCH OF REDNECKS DON'T LIKE "CITY FOLK."
WHICH IS WHY WE'RE GOING WITH YOU. THE MORE GUNS, THE BETTER.

HEY, WE'RE ROLLING OUT IN A COUPLE OF HOURS. WE'RE NOT BABYSITTING HER.
I'LL WATCH HER.

SHE'LL BE SAFE WITH US.
OH... THANKS.
BUT I SHOULD PROBABLY HAVE A GUN, JUST IN CASE.

MILES, WHAT ARE YOU DOING?
I'M RUNNING LOW ON BULLETS SO DON'T SHOOT UNLESS YOU HAVE TO.
I WON'T.

I'LL BE BACK BEFORE YOU KNOW IT.
BUT, DAD...
SHHH, BABY. I'LL BE FINE.

LET'S GO.

I'M THINKING BLUE.
BLUE?
YEAH, I DEFINITELY THINK IT SHOULD BE BLUE.
WHAT THE HELL ARE YOU TALKING ABOUT? WHAT SHOULD BE BLUE?

YOUR CAPE.

SO, WHAT ARE YOU LOOKING AT?
THEM. THEY'RE JUST SITTING A COUPLE MILES OUT, WATCHING US.
WISH I KNEW WHAT THE HELL THEY WERE WAITING FOR.

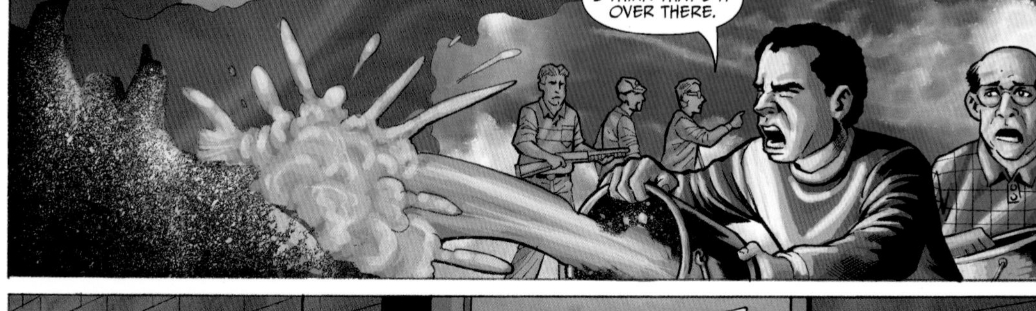
I THINK THAT'S IT OVER THERE.

PHILLIP KLANOWSKI M.D.

HELLO?
ANYBODY HERE?
HEY, DOC!

IS THERE A DOCTOR HERE?
MAYBE HE'S OUT MAKING HOUSE CALLS.
COULD BE HELPING PUT OUT THE FIRE TOO.

WELL, I'M NOT WAITING FOR HIM TO SHOW UP. THERE'S GOT TO BE SOMETHING IN BACK. YOU GUYS KEEP A LOOK OUT.

HOLLER IF YOU GUYS SEE ANYBODY COM--
UH...

EVERYTHING OKAY? WHAT'S... OH.
UM...
IS *THAT* THE DOCTOR?

NO, HE'S NOT THE DOCTOR. JUST PRETENDING TO BE.
DOC, I NEED YOUR HELP. MY--
I'M NOT THE DOCTOR. HE'S DEAD.
DEAD?
HE TRIED TALKING SOME SENSE INTO THAT SHOPKEEPER ACROSS THE WAY. GOT A BULLET IN THE HEAD FOR HIS TROUBLES.
INSULIN. IS THERE ANY HERE?
CHECK THE FRIDGE IN THE BACK. THERE MIGHT BE SOME STERILE SYRINGES BACK THERE TOO.

IS HE YOUR GRANDSON?
NO. HE WAS HERE WHEN I GOT HERE. KEPT TRYING TO HUG ME WHILE I WAS WORKING SO I DRESSED HIM UP TO KEEP HIM ENTERTAINED.

DOESN'T SEEM TO BE WORKING THOUGH.
OH, HEY! HEH HEH. WHAT'S YOUR NAME, LITTLE GUY?

HE DOESN'T TALK. AUTISTIC I THINK. AND I HAVE NO IDEA WHAT HIS NAME IS. DOCTOR WAS KILLED BEFORE HE MENTIONED IT.
SO ARE YOU A NURSE?

NOT CERTIFIED, BUT CLOSE ENOUGH.

YOU FIND WHAT YOU NEED?
YES, THANK GOD. SO UNLESS YOU NEED SOME BAND-AIDS, LET'S GET THE HELL OUT OF HERE.
YOU AIN'T GOING ANYWHERE.

SEE, SHERIFF? TOLD YOU I SAW LOOTERS COMING IN HERE.
THAT YOU DID.
AND THAT'S A PROBLEM.

YOU SEE, MY JAIL'S FULL, I DON'T HAVE ANYTHING TO FEED YOU, AND THE LOCAL JUDGE IS BURIED UNDER WHAT'S LEFT OF THE COURTHOUSE.
ALL OF WHICH LEADS ME TO ASK THE QUESTION...

WHAT THE HELL AM I GONNA DO WITH YOU?
NEXT ISSUE: NEW AMERICA

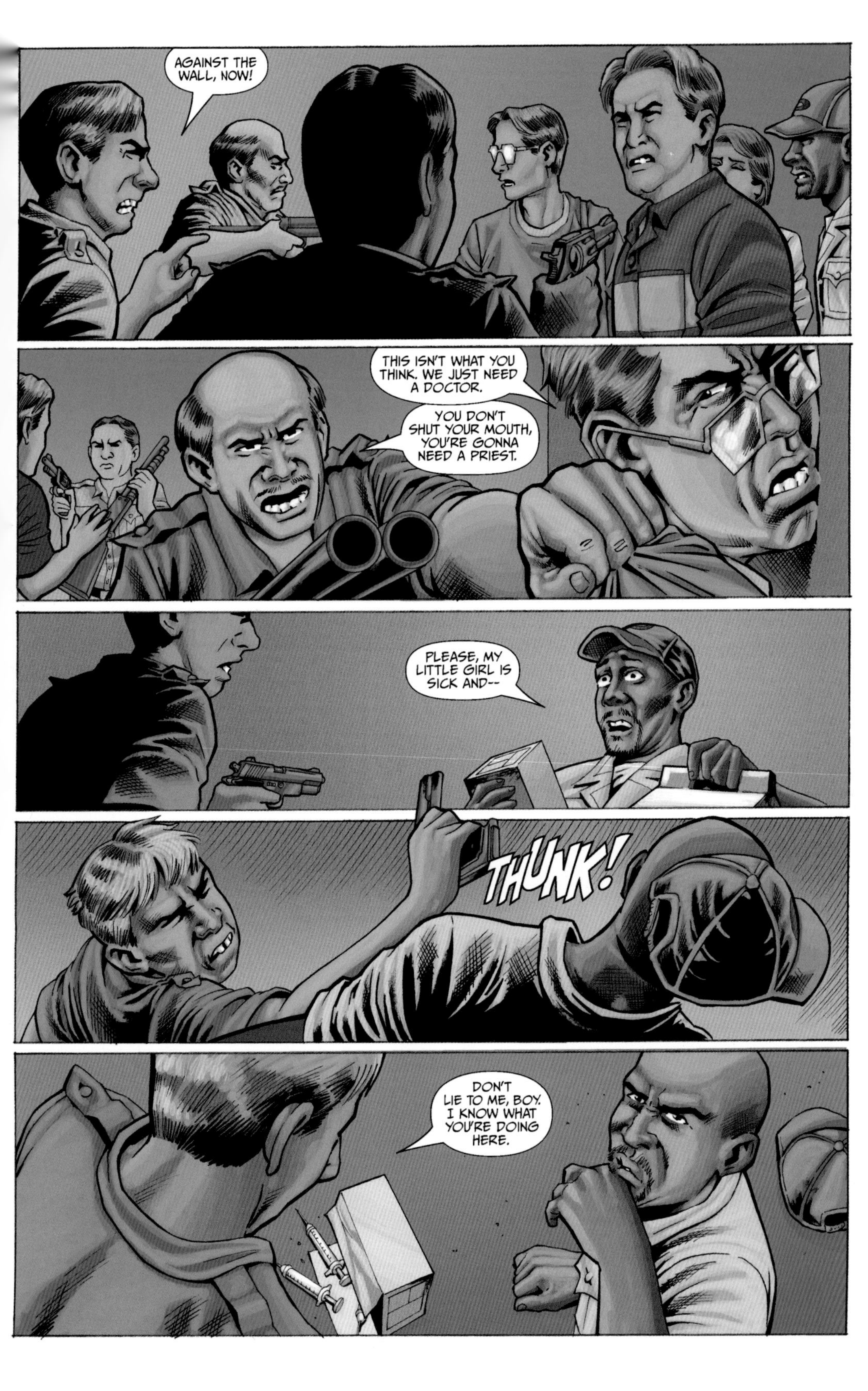
AGAINST THE WALL, NOW!
THIS ISN'T WHAT YOU THINK. WE JUST NEED A DOCTOR.
YOU DON'T SHUT YOUR MOUTH, YOU'RE GONNA NEED A PRIEST.
PLEASE, MY LITTLE GIRL IS SICK AND--
THUNK!
DON'T LIE TO ME, BOY. I KNOW WHAT YOU'RE DOING HERE.

WHAT'S HE GOT THERE?
AS I FIGURED. NEEDLES. AND WHAT LOOKS LIKE MORPHINE.
GUESS WE GOT OURSELVES A JUNKIE.

IT'S INSULIN YOU STUPID HILLBILLY.

YOU BACK TALKIN' ME YOU SON OF A--
THAT'S ENOUGH, CLINT. JUST CUFF HIM.

WHAT'S YOUR PART IN THIS, MA'AM?
TRAVELING UP FROM THE RED LINE WITH A PATIENT. DR. KLANOWSKI WAS LETTING ME USE HIS FACILITIES.
BUT THEN SOMEONE, YOU KNOW, SHOT HIM.

AND THAT MAN IS TELLING THE TRUTH. HE CAME HERE FOR INSULIN.
I DON'T CARE IF HE CAME FOR LOLLIPOPS. NOBODY STEALS IN MY TOWN.

MY GIRL'S DYING!
TELL IT TO YOUR LAWYER.
HEH HEH HEH...

WHERE'S THIS PATIENT OF YOURS?
IN THE BACK.
I'LL CHECK IT OUT.

ARE YOU A NURSE?
NO, BUT CLOSE ENOUGH FOR GOVERNMENT WORK.
WHAT THE HELL?

HEY SHERIFF, YOU GOT TO SEE THIS.

GESUNDHEIT.
NEW AMERICA
MICHAEL ALAN NELSON WRITER
CHEE ARTIST
ED DUKESHIRE LETTERER
MATT WEBB COLORIST
MARSHALL DILLON MANAGING EDITOR

YOU ALWAYS KEEP YOUR PATIENTS HANDCUFFED TO THEIR BEDS?
ONLY THE DANGEROUS ONES.
WHAT'S WRONG WITH HIM?

I'M A *REAL* JUNKIE.

DON'T SWEAT IT, BARNEY FIFE. IT'S JUST A LITTLE HONEY TO KEEP THE BEES FROM BUZZING.

WHAT'S YOUR NAME, SON?
CITY PARRISH, DAD.
WISE ASS, EH?
GET HIM OFF THAT BED. HE'S COMING WITH US.

WITH ALL DUE RESPECT, THIS MAN IS UNDER MY CARE.
AND NOW HE'S UNDER MINE.

SHERIFF, YOU DON'T UNDERSTAND. HE NEEDS CONSTANT MEDICAL SUPERVISION.
NO, *YOU* DON'T UNDERSTAND.

YOU'RE NOT WASTING ANY MORE OF MY MEDICINE ON SOME STRUNG-OUT CRACK-HEAD. BESIDES...
...YOU'VE GOT A NEW PATIENT.

YOUR MOVE.
I'M THINKING.
YOU'RE EXES, REMEMBER.

NUH UH. STOP CHEATING.
WELL HOW ELSE AM I GOING TO WIN?

SO DID YOU REALLY GET TO SEE ONE? LIKE, UP CLOSE?
MMM HMMM.
IS IT TRUE THEY LOOK LIKE SQUID?
SORT OF. MORE LIKE AN OCTOPUS, I GUESS. OR THOSE CUTTLEFISH THINGIES.

YEAH, I SAW THOSE AT THE AQUARIUM ONCE WITH MY MOM. SHE DIDN'T LIKE THEM, THOUGH. SHE LIKED THE ONES WITH ALL THE PRETTY COLORS.

WHY AREN'T THEY ATTACKING US?
DON'T KNOW. THEY SEEM TO BE STICKING TO JUST THE CITIES THIS TIME AROUND.
SO IT'S SAFE HERE? THEY WON'T COME AFTER US HERE?

I DON'T KNOW. HONESTLY, YOU KNOW JUST AS MUCH AS WE DO.
WELL, WHAT ABOUT THE PRESIDENT? WHAT DID HE SAY WE SHOULD DO?
PRESIDENT? HEH. WHICH ONE? WE'VE GOT, WHAT...THREE OF THEM NOW?
AT LEAST.

WHAT?
YEAH, SURVIVING POLITICIANS GOT PRETTY NASTY AFTER THE DYING. I MEAN, THE SECRETARY OF STATE BEAT THE MINORITY LEADER INTO A COMA.
PAST TWO WEEKS HAVE BEEN CRAZY. HELL, KANSAS SAYS THEY'RE NOT EVEN PART OF THE UNION ANY MORE.

BUT THE LINE OF SUCCESSION. WHO'S IN CHARGE?
HEY, SERGEANT!

I THINK THEY'RE GETTING READY TO DO SOMETHING.

GET HIM UP ON THAT BED.
SHERIFF, I TOLD YOU. I'M NOT A DOCTOR.

WELL, YOU'RE THE CLOSEST THING I'VE GOT. SO GET TO IT.
THAT MAN HAS THIRD DEGREE BURNS OVER NINETY PERCENT OF HIS BODY. WHAT EXACTLY DO YOU EXPECT ME TO DO?

SAVE HIM. HE TRIED TO KEEP OUR FOOD FROM BURNING. THAT MAN'S A HERO.
THAT MAN'S A CHARCOAL BRIQUETTE!
THAT MAN IS MY BROTHER.

CLINT, STAY WITH HER. MAKE SURE SHE DOES HER JOB.

LET'S GO.

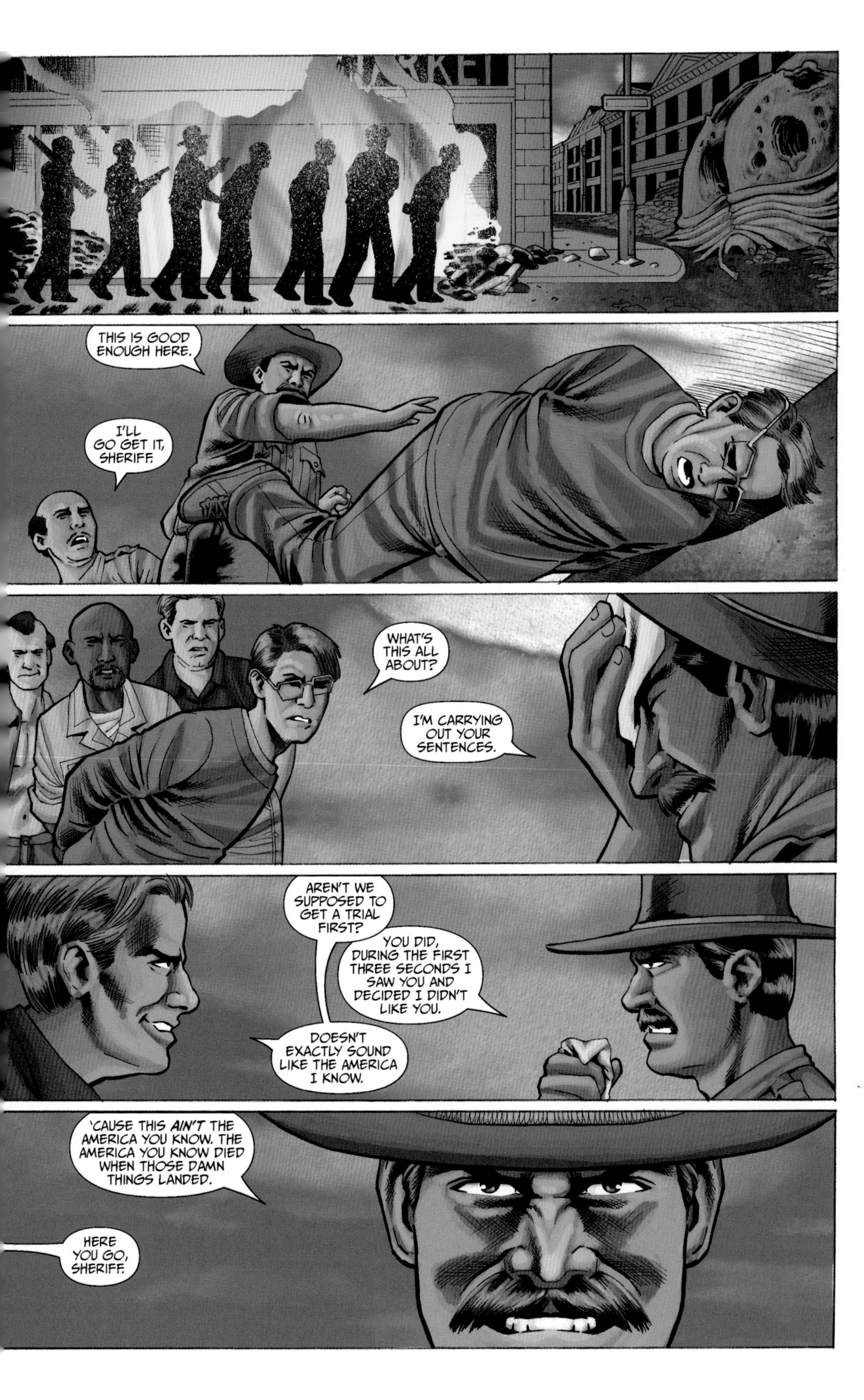

ARKET
THIS IS GOOD ENOUGH HERE.
I'LL GO GET IT, SHERIFF.
WHAT'S THIS ALL ABOUT?
I'M CARRYING OUT YOUR SENTENCES.
AREN'T WE SUPPOSED TO GET A TRIAL FIRST?
YOU DID, DURING THE FIRST THREE SECONDS I SAW YOU AND DECIDED I DIDN'T LIKE YOU.
DOESN'T EXACTLY SOUND LIKE THE AMERICA I KNOW.
'CAUSE THIS *AIN'T* THE AMERICA YOU KNOW. THE AMERICA YOU KNOW DIED WHEN THOSE DAMN THINGS LANDED.
HERE YOU GO, SHERIFF.

SO LET ME INTRODUCE YOU TO THE *NEW* AMERICA.

WHAT'S THAT?
JUST SOMETHING TO HELP HIM SLEEP.

YOU SHOULD PROBABLY PUT SOME ALOE ON HIM.

ALOE.
YOU KNOW, THAT STUFF YOU USE FOR SUNBURNS.
...
LET'S SEE HOW THE ANTIBIOTICS TAKE FIRST, OKAY?

WHERE ARE YOU GOING?
TO GET SOME COFFEE. I'M DEAD ON MY FEET. YOU WANT SOME?

YOU TAKE CREAM AND SUGAR?
WHAT ARE YOU LOOKING AT, RETARD?

HELL NO. ONLY PANSIES DRINK--HEY! GET OFF ME!

HE'S JUST REALLY AFFECTIONATE.
HE'S WEIRD IS WHAT HE IS. HE'S NOT CONTAGIOUS OR ANYTHING IS HE?
I DOUBT IT. MUST HAVE LOST HIS FAMILY. SO THE DOCTOR MUST HAVE BEEN TAKING CARE OF HIM.

FIGURES. THAT OLD MAN WAS ALWAYS TRYING TO HELP THE WRONG PEOPLE. NOW THE SHERIFF'S BROTHER'S GOT NO DOCTOR.
TRUE, BUT IT DOESN'T REALLY MATTER. THE SHERIFF'S BROTHER DOESN'T NEED A DOCTOR.
SO HE'S GOING TO BE OKAY?

OF COURSE NOT. THE MAN'S DEAD.
HOW'S YOUR COFFEE?

WHAT ARE THEY DOING?
NOT SURE. SOMETHING WITH ONE OF THE D.O.A.S.
D.O.A.S?
DEAD ON ARRIVAL. A LOT OF THE ALIEN MACHINES THAT LANDED IN THE SECOND WAVE WERE D.O.A.

ALRIGHT, LET'S MOVE!
WAIT, YOU'RE LEAVING? BUT WHAT ARE THEY DOING?
MA'AM, I DON'T KNOW. I'M SORRY. NOW, WE'VE GOT ORDERS TO MOVE OUT. I SUGGEST YOU DO THE SAME.

WHAT'S GOING ON?
I HAVE NO IDEA. AND APPARENTLY, NEITHER DOES ANYONE ELSE.
BUT WE CAN'T STAY HERE. THE ALIENS ARE UP TO SOMETHING AND I DON'T THINK WE SHOULD STICK AROUND TO FIND OUT WHAT IT IS.

RONNI, HOW ARE YOU FEELING?
TIRED. AND THIRSTY. REALLY THIRSTY.
I KNOW. HANG IN THERE. HANG IN THERE. YOU'RE GOING TO GET YOUR MEDICINE SOON. NOW COME ON.
WE SHOULD GO FIND YOUR DAD.

HEY, DO YOU HEAR SOMETHING?

SSSSHHHCCCCCSSSSSHHHHHCCCSSSSSCCCCCSHHHH
HAVE YOU LOST YOUR MIND? WE HAVE LAWS IN THIS COUNTRY. LAWS YOU'RE SUPPOSED TO UPHOLD! DUE PROCESS!
I DON'T KNOW IF YOU'VE NOTICED, BUT UNCLE SAM AIN'T AROUND ANY MORE TO GIVE YOU YOUR ***DUE PROCESS.*** WHICH MAKES ***ME*** THE LAW.
EVER SINCE THOSE ALIENS CAME, EVERY KIND OF CITY FILTH HAS BEEN POURING INTO MY TOWN.

r3d h34dz
rool
SHACK
"LOOTERS, JUNKIES, VANDALS, FREAKS. THE ALIENS CAME AND FLUSHED THAT URBAN TOILET RIGHT INTO MY BACKYARD."
"WELL I'M NOT HAVING IT. YOU TRIED TO STEAL FROM ME AND MINE. I WON'T LET THAT STAND."

YOU KNOW, I'VE ACTUALLY BEEN FLUSHED DOWN A TOILET BEFORE AND I CAN SEE YOUR POINT. THIS TOWN IS JUST LIKE THAT. IT LOOKS BAD, SMELLS WORSE...
AND I'M SURROUNDED BY PIECES OF S--

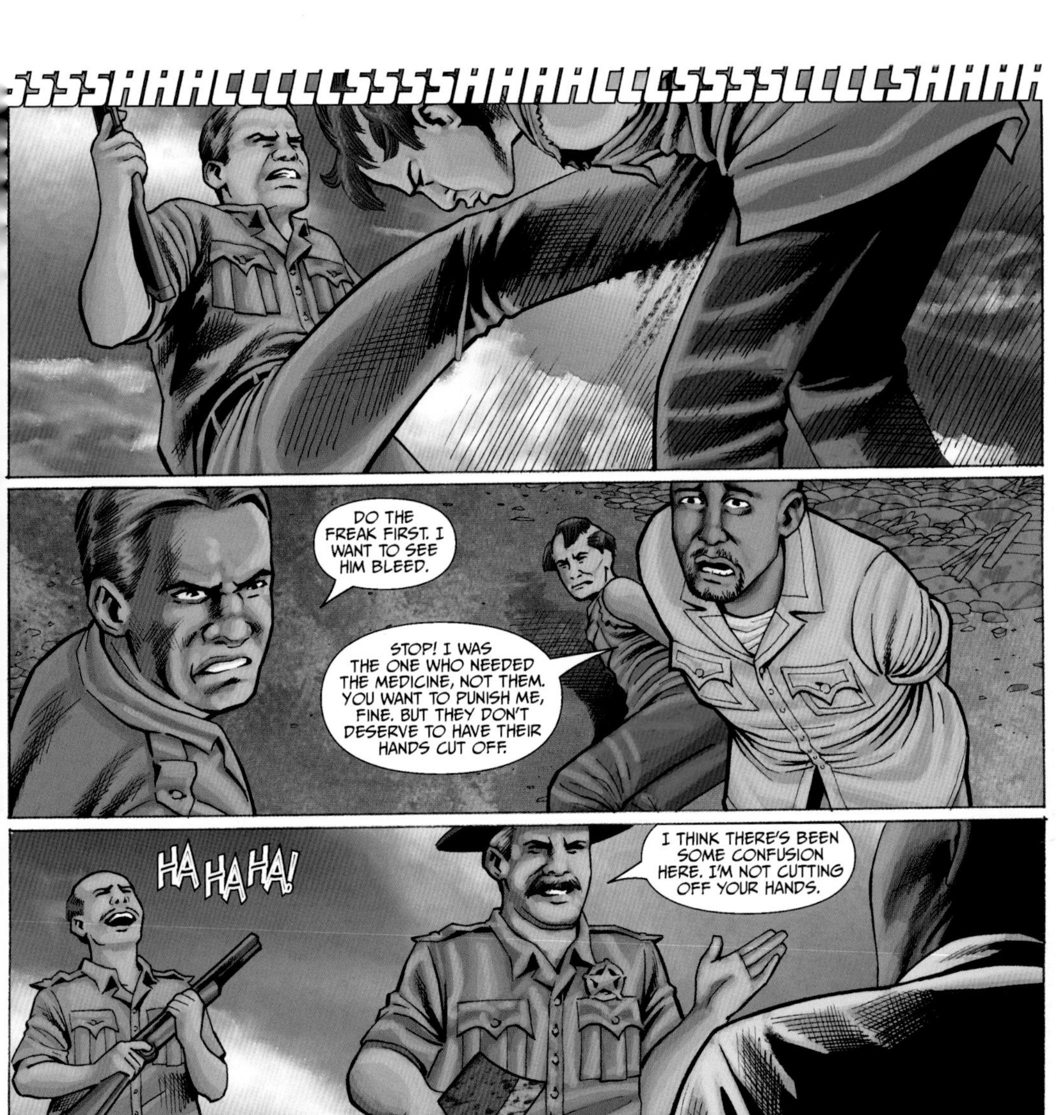
SSSSHHHLLLLLSSSSHHHHLLLSSSSLLLLSHHHH
DO THE FREAK FIRST. I WANT TO SEE HIM BLEED.
STOP! I WAS THE ONE WHO NEEDED THE MEDICINE, NOT THEM. YOU WANT TO PUNISH ME, FINE. BUT THEY DON'T DESERVE TO HAVE THEIR HANDS CUT OFF.

HA HA HA!
I THINK THERE'S BEEN SOME CONFUSION HERE. I'M NOT CUTTING OFF YOUR HANDS.

I'M CUTTING OFF YOUR HEADS.
WHY WASTE BULLETS IF I DON'T HAVE TO?

WHAT DO YOU MEAN HE'S DEAD?
DEAD. AS IN NOT ALIVE. I GAVE HIM A COMBINATION OF PAIN KILLER AND MUSCLE RELAXANT. LETHAL DOSE. HE DIED ALMOST INSTANTLY.
...

YOU STUPID BITCH. YOU'RE GONNA GET BACK IN THERE AND DO WHAT THE SHERIFF TOLD YOU!
NO, I'M NOT. IT WAS A MERCY, BELIEVE ME. EVEN IF HE WAS IN THE BEST BURN CARE CENTER IN THE COUNTRY, HE WOULD HAVE BEEN DEAD IN A WEEK.
WHAT HAVE YOU DONE?! WHAT THE HELL...HAVE YOU...WHAT DID YOU...

WHAT...WHY DO I FEEL...FEEL LIKE...ALL...DID YOU DRUG...THE COFFEE?
DON'T BE SILLY. THIS IS SOME OF THE LAST COFFEE WE'RE EVER LIKELY TO HAVE. I WOULD NEVER DO SUCH A HORRIBLE THING AS RUIN IT.

SO I PUT IT ON THE CUP HANDLE INSTEAD.

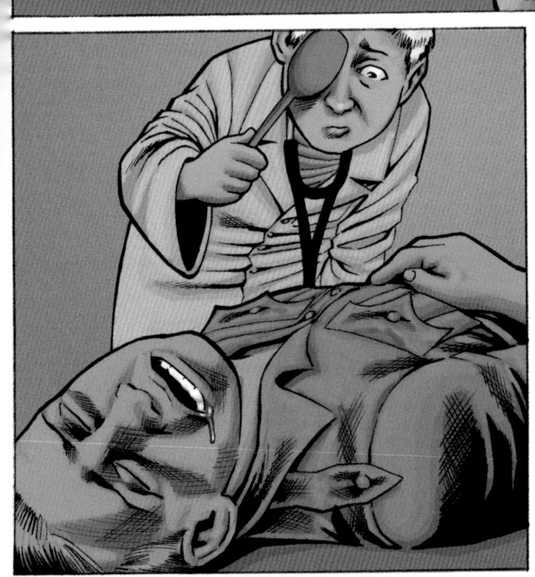

COME ON, YOUNG MAN. I GUESS I CAN'T LEAVE YOU HERE, CAN I?

SSSHHHCCCCSSSSHHHCCCSSSCCCSHHHH

SSSSHHHCCCCCCSSSSSHHHHCCCSSSSCCCCSHHHH
GIRLS, STAY CLOSE, OKAY?
ROBS

MISS JANE, I'M SORRY, BUT COULD WE STOP FOR A MINUTE? I JUST NEED TO REST.
OKAY, BUT JUST FOR A MINUTE.

YOU'RE DOING GREAT, RONNI.
THANKS, CORA. I JUST WISH I DIDN'T HAVE TO BE SICK.
I DON'T LIKE IT WHEN MY DAD HAS TO LEAVE TO FIND MEDICINE.

WE'RE GOING TO FIND HIM REALLY SOON, DON'T YOU WORRY.
OH MY GOD. THERE HE IS.

STAY HERE. STAY WITH THE BAG AND I'LL BE RIGHT BACK.
GOD, I SURE HOPE YOU UNDERSTAND WHAT I'M SAYING.

SSSSSCCCCCCRRRRRRRREEEEEEEEEEESSSSSHHHHHH
ON YOUR KNEES FREAK!
YOU CAN'T DO THIS! YOU CRAZY BASTARDS! YOU CAN'T--
DAD?

WHOOOM!

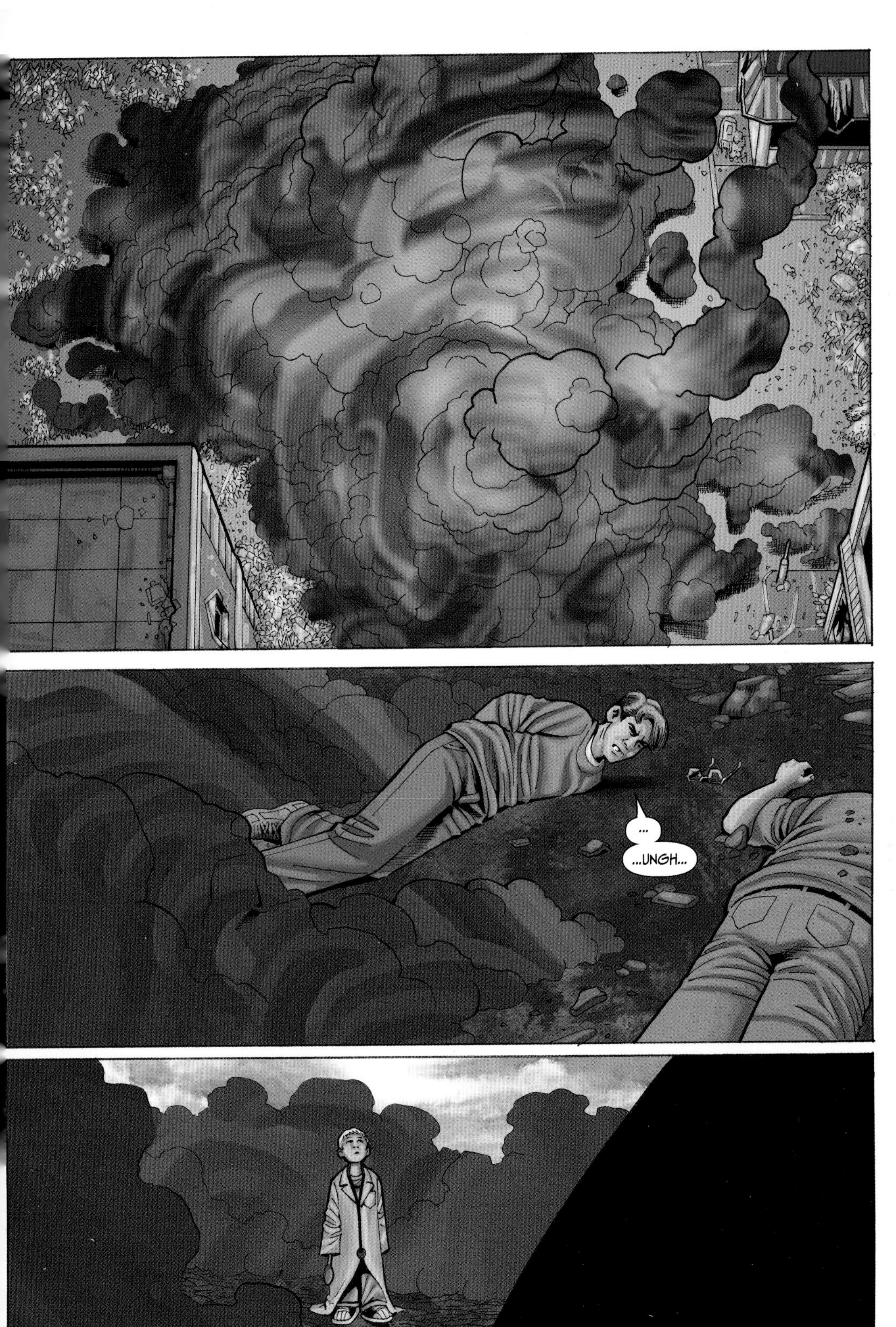
...
...UNGH...

NEXT ISSUE:
SMOKIN' RED HEAD.

MILES, ARE YOU AWAKE?
NO.
LIAR.
SCOUT'S HONOR. I'M FAST ASLEEP.
REALLY? WELL, PARTS OF YOU ARE WIDE AWAKE.
LEAVE MY PARTS ALONE.
COME BACK HERE WITH THE SHEETS, YOU SAUCY TART! IT'S COLD!
AHH! STOP TICKLING ME!
AHH! HA HA! STOP IT! STOP! AHH!
SMOKIN' RED HEAD
MICHAEL ALAN NELSON WRITER
CHEE ARTIST
ED DUKESHIRE LETTERER
MATT WEBB COLORIST
MARSHALL DILLON MANAGING EDITOR
ALWAYS STEALING THE COVERS.
I THINK I KNOW HOW TO WARM YOU UP.
MILES!

IT'S DUKE. HE WANTS YOU TO GO.
I WISH HE'D JUST GO AWAY. WHY CAN'T HE JUST LEAVE US ALONE?
HE WOULDN'T BE MUCH OF A FRIEND IF HE DID. GO ON, HE'S WAITING.
SO LET HIM WAIT.
MILES, WHAT ARE YOU DOING? YOU DON'T BELONG HERE, NOW LET'S GO.
I DIDN'T KNOW YOU SMOKED.
I DON'T, SILLY. I'M A BRUNETTE, NOT A RED HEAD. NOW GO, MILES. DON'T KEEP HIM WAITING.
GINA, YOU'RE NOT MAKING ANY SENSE. NOW PUT SOME CLOTHES ON BEFORE YOU CATCH PNEUMONIA.
WHY'S IT SO DAMN COLD IN HERE, ANYWAY?
MILES, HONEY...
IT'S ALWAYS COLD HERE IN THE DARK.
WELL, I'M NOT GOING ANYWHERE WITH-OUT YOU.
LIAR.

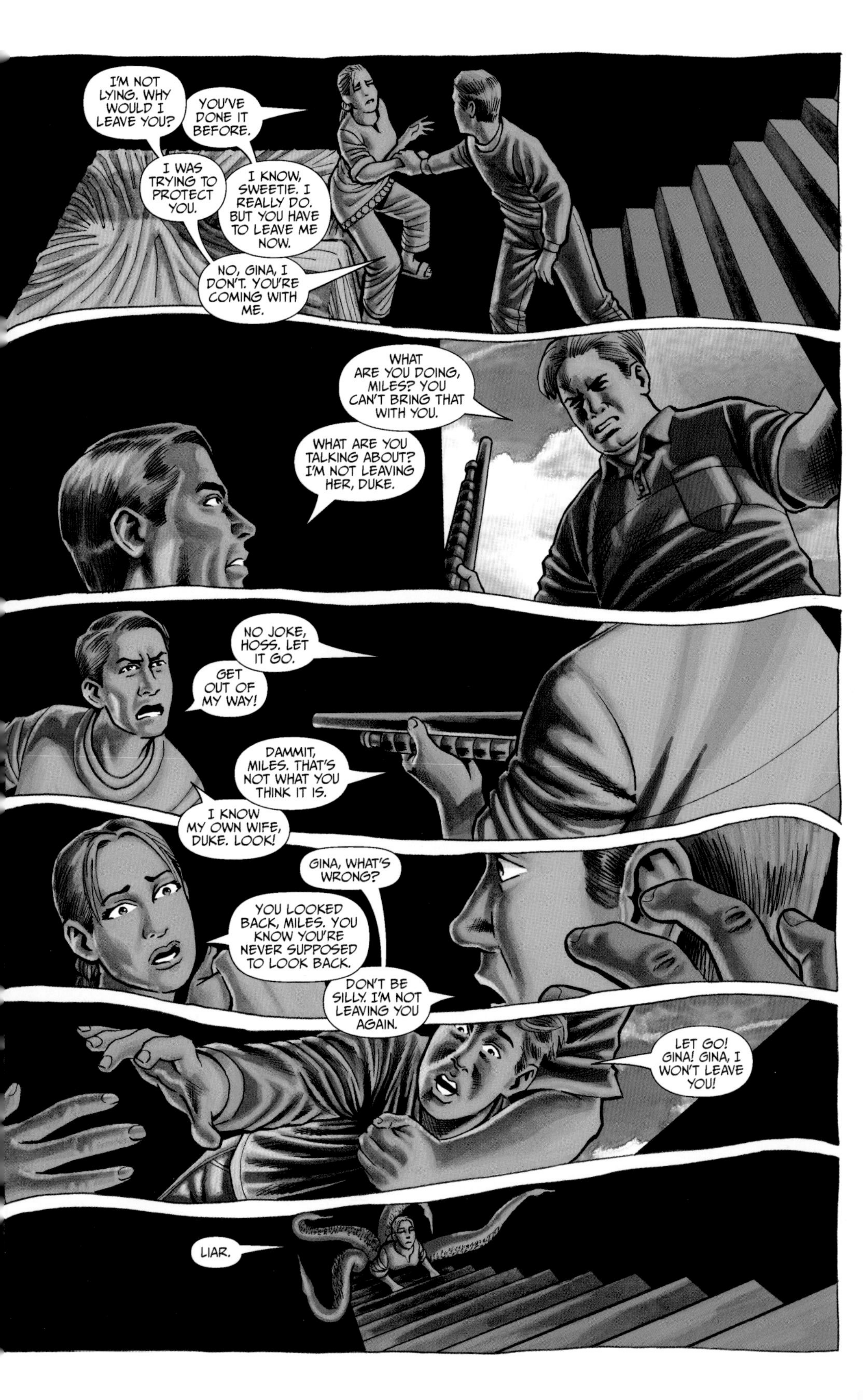
I'M NOT LYING. WHY WOULD I LEAVE YOU?
YOU'VE DONE IT BEFORE.
I WAS TRYING TO PROTECT YOU.
I KNOW, SWEETIE. I REALLY DO. BUT YOU HAVE TO LEAVE ME NOW.
NO, GINA, I DON'T. YOU'RE COMING WITH ME.
WHAT ARE YOU DOING, MILES? YOU CAN'T BRING THAT WITH YOU.
WHAT ARE YOU TALKING ABOUT? I'M NOT LEAVING HER, DUKE.
NO JOKE, HOSS. LET IT GO.
GET OUT OF MY WAY!
DAMMIT, MILES. THAT'S NOT WHAT YOU THINK IT IS.
I KNOW MY OWN WIFE, DUKE. LOOK!
GINA, WHAT'S WRONG?
YOU LOOKED BACK, MILES. YOU KNOW YOU'RE NEVER SUPPOSED TO LOOK BACK.
DON'T BE SILLY. I'M NOT LEAVING YOU AGAIN.
LET GO! GINA! GINA, I WON'T LEAVE YOU!
LIAR.

MILES, WAKE UP. COME ON, HOSS.
GINA... LET GO... LEAVE... GINA...

WH...DUKE? WHAT THE HELL HAPPENED?
DAMN SQUIDDY DROPPED ON OUR HEADS. WE GOT LUCKY THOUGH. IT'S ONE OF THOSE D.O.A.S.
NOW HOLD STILL SO I CAN UNCUFF YOU.
IS ANYONE HURT?

RONNI!
I'M OKAY, DAD.

SOMEONE WITH KEYS WANT TO DO ME SOLID SO I CAN HUG MY GIRL?
I GOT YOU, RIGHT HERE.
I'LL CHECK ON THE OTHERS.

JANE, CORA, YOU OKAY?
JUST A LITTLE SHAKEN. IS THAT ONE OF THOSE D--

MILES, LOOK OUT!

MILES!
FILTHY... SON OF A...

STAY BEHIND ME, BABY. I DON'T--
...HUNH...

DON'T LOOK, RONNI.

OOOF!

WHO'D YOU THINK YOU WERE MESSING WITH, BOY?

BLAM!

THANKS.
UM...YOU WERE AIMING FOR HIM, RIGHT?

I'M GOING TO SEE IF ANYONE ELSE NEEDS HELP.

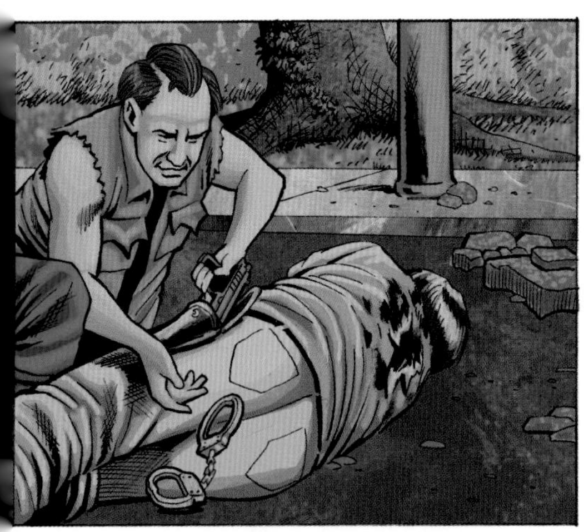

CITY?

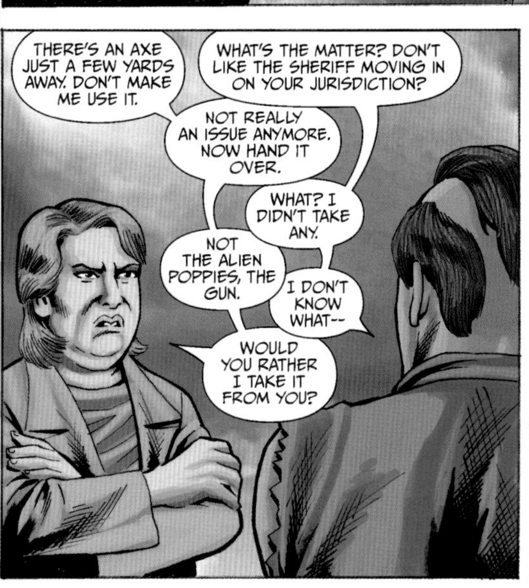
THERE'S AN AXE JUST A FEW YARDS AWAY. DON'T MAKE ME USE IT.
WHAT'S THE MATTER? DON'T LIKE THE SHERIFF MOVING IN ON YOUR JURISDICTION?
NOT REALLY AN ISSUE ANYMORE. NOW HAND IT OVER.
WHAT? I DIDN'T TAKE ANY.
NOT THE ALIEN POPPIES, THE GUN.
I DON'T KNOW WHAT--
WOULD YOU RATHER I TAKE IT FROM YOU?

SMART BOY.
YOU CAN'T KEEP ME SOBER FOREVER, YOU KNOW.
I'VE BROUGHT YOU THIS FAR, CITY. YOU DON'T WANT TO FALL OF THE WAGON NOW.

ARE YOU OKAY?
I'M FINE.
MOM. YOU JUST SHOT A COP.
COME ON, YOUNG MAN. COME AWAY FROM THERE.
ARE YOU LISTENING TO ME?

YES, CORA. I CAN HEAR YOU.
WELL?
WELL...YOUR MOTHER'S NOT PERFECT. IT'S ABOUT TIME YOU LEARNED THAT.
NOT PERFECT? MOM, WE'RE NOT TALKING ABOUT DRINKING TOO MUCH WINE AT DINNER OR CHEATING ON YOUR TAXES.
YOU JUST KILLED A MAN!

YES I DID, AFTER AN *ALIEN SPACESHIP* NEARLY CRUSHED US TO DEATH! ALIENS, CORA. I'VE BEEN A LITTLE CONFUSED EVER SINCE ONE OF THEM *ATE* MY HUSBAND, SO FORGIVE ME IF I SEEM A LITTLE OUT OF CHARACTER TO YOU.
I'M SORRY, I JUST...

YOU'RE SCARING ME.
YEAH, WELL I'M SCARING ME TOO.

WELL, THIS LITTLE FELLA ISN'T SCARED. ARE YOU? DO YOU HAVE A NAME? I'M JANE AND THIS IS MY DAUGHTER, CORA.
DON'T WANT TO TALK? THAT'S OKAY.
EVERYTHING'S GOING TO BE OKAY.

IS THIS YOUR DAUGHTER?
RONNI.
HI, RONNI. I'M GLADYS. YOU'RE A TYPE ONE DIABETIC, RIGHT?
YES, MA'AM.
WELL DON'T YOU WORRY. WE'RE GOING TO HAVE YOU RIGHT AS RAIN IN NO TIME.

WHO'S HE?
HIS NAME IS CITY PARRISH.
SHOULDN'T HE BE IN HANDCUFFS OR SOMETHING?
NO, THAT'S NOT NECESSARY. BUT IF HE THREATENS YOU OR LITTLE RONNI HERE, YOU HAVE MY PERMISSION TO SHOOT HIM.
REPEATEDLY.
AHH, YOU REMIND ME SO MUCH OF MY GRANDMOTHER BEFORE THE BLESSED CANCER KILLED HER.

D.O.A. DAMN, I DON'T THINK I'VE EVER BEEN THIS LUCKY BEFORE.
DON'T BUY YOURSELF A LOTTERY TICKET JUST YET. DOESN'T THIS LOOK... STRANGE TO YOU?
YEAH. BUT MOST THINGS FROM OUTER SPACE KINDA DO.
I MEAN IT DOESN'T LOOK LIKE A TRIPOD. IT DOESN'T EVEN HAVE LEGS.

WELL, AS MUCH AS I'D LOVE TO PLAY C.S.I. MARS WITH YOU MILES, WE SHOULD SKIP OUT BEFORE THE LOCALS COME OUT OF HIDING AND SEE WE KILLED THEIR LAW MAN.
GOD I NEED A CHEW.
YOU KNOW, DUKE, YOU REALLY... OUGHT TO... QUIT...

r3d h34dz r00l
GESUNDHEIT

IS THAT TRIPOD GLOWING?
OH GOD.

WE NEED TO GET EVERYONE BACK TO THE TRACTOR.
MILES, WHAT THE HELL IS GOING ON?
THAT TRIPOD IS GLOWING.
DON'T THEY ALL?
NOT THE DEAD ONES.
NOT SURE WHAT YOU'RE GETTING AT, HOSS.

YOU REMEMBER WHEN THOSE TRIPODS CHASED US THROUGH THE PASTURE, RIGHT? WHEN THE ONE GOT OUT AHEAD OF THE OTHER TWO, WHAT HAPPENED?
UM, THE CRAZY ALIENS GOT TRIGGER HAPPY AND FRIED IT.
THAT'S RIGHT. AND JUST BEFORE THEY FRIED IT, IT LOOKED LIKE ALL THE DEAD ONES LEFT FROM THE FIRST WAVE. DULL, LIKE GRAY PLASTIC. NOW LOOK!

THEY KILLED IT BECAUSE IT BECAME CONTAMINATED. THESE THINGS THAT HAVE BEEN LANDING AREN'T D.O.A. THEY'RE NOT TRIPODS AT ALL!
THEY'RE SCRUBBERS THAT CLEAN THE AIR. WHEN THE AIR IS SAFE, THE TRIPODS GLOW.
r3d h34dz r00l
SO OUR GERMS REALLY DID KILL THEM OFF.

NO. IF THAT WAS TRUE, THEY PROBABLY WOULD HAVE GOTTEN SICK AFTER ABDUCTING ME AND ANYONE ELSE THEY TOOK LONG BEFORE THEY LANDED.
NO, THIS DEFINITELY RIDS THE AIR FROM GERMS, BUT NOT FROM OURS.
SO WHAT ARE YOU SAYING?

I'M SAYING THAT THEY WERE SICK BEFORE THEY EVEN GOT HERE.

EVERYBODY LISTEN. WE HAVE TO GET OUT OF HERE NOW.
CAPTAIN UNDERSTATEMENT HAS A POINT.
BUT IT'S D.O.A. WHY THE SUDDEN URGENCY?
IT'S NOT A TRIPOD. IT'S A SCRUBBER. SCRUBS THE AIR, LIKE ONE OF THOSE IONIZERS YOU CAN BUY IN AIRPLANE MAGAZINES. YOU KNOW, GETS RID OF CIGAR AND DOG--
STOP TALKING.
ALIENS ARE COMING TO TOWN AND'LL BE HERE ANY MINUTE. WE'VE GOT A TRACTOR WITH A FLATBED THAT CAN HOLD ALL OF US. BUT TRAIN'S LEAVING THE STATION IN TEN.
IS THIS YOUR GRANDSON? HE WON'T TALK TO ME.
NO, HE'S A LOCAL. NO FAMILY.
SHOULD WE TAKE HIM WITH US?
I'M NOT LEAVING *ANYONE* BEHIND. HE'S COMING WITH US.

THEY'RE STILL WAITING.
THE SCRUBBER'S RANGE HAS TO BE LIMITED. WE'LL HAVE TO DRIVE UNTIL WE'RE OUT OF IT.
SOUNDS LIKE A PLAN.
BUT IT'S SPREADING TOO FAST. I DON'T THINK WE'LL HAVE TIME TO GO AROUND THE TOWN.
THEN I GUESS YOU BETTER HOLD ON TO SOMETHING.

THIS IS THE MOST PATHETIC GET-AWAY VEHICLE EVER.
YOU'RE MORE THAN WELCOME TO WALK.
OKAY.
SIT DOWN.
HOW YOU FEELING, BABY?
BETTER. THANKS, DAD.

STAY AWAY FROM THE EDGE, NOW.
DUKE! THEY'RE COMING!

CRAAACK!!
HANG ON!
CRASH!
CORA!
GO! DON'T STOP!
KEEP GOING!
FEEL THE NEED, FARM BOY!
DAMMIT, MILES.

OH GOD, I THINK THEY SEE US.
GOOD.

GOOD? GOOD?!
HOW THE HELL ARE WE GOING TO DO THAT?
WE MIGHT BE ABLE TO DISTRACT THEM LONG ENOUGH TO LET THE OTHERS GET AWAY.
BY PLAYING A GAME OF "KING OF THE HILL."

WE HAVE TO GET HIGHER.
IT'S SLIPPERY.
YOU CAN DO IT, KEEP GOING.
I CAN'T HOLD ON!
GRAB ON TO ME AND DON'T LET GO.
THEY'RE GOING TO SEE US UP HERE.
THAT'S THE POINT. THEY CAN'T SHOOT US WITHOUT SHOOTING THE SCRUBBER, SO WE SHOULD BE SAFE.
SHOULD BE?!
THUNK!

WELL, NOW WE'RE GOING TO FIND OUT.

C'MON, YOU THREE-LEGGED BASTARDS! COME GET SOME!
OH GOD YOU'RE A CRAZY MAN.
SLAM! SLAM!

THAT'S RIGHT, C'MON! BRING IT! LET'S SEE WHAT YOU'RE MADE OF!

AFRAID TO SHOOT ME, IS THAT IT? DON'T WANT TO DAMAGE YOUR LITTLE TOY? COME ON, DO IT! SHOOT ME! SHOOT ME!

MILES! THEIR TENTACLES!

OH...
GUESS I SHOULD HAVE THOUGHT OF THAT.

SLIDE!
AHHH!
BOB'S STATION
THEY'RE FOLLOWING US!
I KNOW, I KNOW! QUICK, OVER HERE!
CRAASH!
BOOOM!
RRRRRRRRRRRRRR!

CORA! COOORAAAAA!!!
EASY, JANE. EASY.
OVER THERE. THERE'S AN OLD TRIPOD THAT'S NOT GLOWING.
WE'LL GO A LITTLE FURTHER PAST JUST TO MAKE SURE. THEN WE'LL STOP.
DAD, IS...IS CORA GOING TO BE OKAY? I REALLY LIKED HER.
WE'LL WAIT FOR A WHILE. SEE IF THEY MEET UP WITH US.
I DON'T KNOW, BABY.
IT'S COMING!
I SEE IT, I SEE IT.
COME ON, WHERE THE HELL IS SECOND GEAR?!
WHAT?!
AHHH! IT'S HOT, IT'S HOT!
ZZZZHHHHHIIITTTTTT!
FOUND IT! HANG ON!
KEERAAAAAACK!!!

HEY LOOK! SOMETHING'S COMING.
IT'S THEM! QUICK, LET THEM KNOW IT'S SAFE OVER HERE!

HERE! MILES, OVER HERE!
HEY! HEY!
CORA! CORA!
HURRY UP AND GET OVER HERE!
THIS WAY!
YES, BY ALL MEANS, LEAD THE ALIENS DIRECTLY *TOWARD US.*

I SEE THEM! OVER THERE!

OH, CORA. DON'T YOU EVER SCARE YOUR MOTHER LIKE THAT AGAIN!
MILES, YOU ARE ONE LUCKY SON OF A BITCH!
GUESS NOW WOULD BE A GOOD TIME TO BUY THAT LOTTERY TICKET, HUH?
COME ON, WE'RE STILL A LITTLE TOO CLOSE. LET'S FIND THE NEXT FIRST WAVE TRIPOD AND MAKE CAMP FOR THE NIGHT.

WHY DON'T YOU COME TO THE FIRE SO I CAN HAVE A LOOK.
IT'S JUST A SCRATCH, I'LL BE FINE.
CITY, WE'RE LOW ON ANTIBIOTICS. I'D RATHER AVOID IT GETTING INFECTED. SO TAKE OFF YOUR SHIRT AND COME TO THE FIRE.
LET ME SMOKE FIRST.
EXCUSE ME?
A *CIGARETTE*, YOU PARANOID COW.
WELL, HURRY UP. IT'S FREEZING.
I THOUGHT THEY TAUGHT YOU HOW TO BRAVE THE ELEMENTS IN SPOOK CAMP.
YES, THEY ALSO TAUGHT ME OTHER THINGS. THINGS WITH STICKS. THINGS I'M GOING TO SHOW YOU IF YOU DON'T GET TO IT.
OH, I BET YOU WERE THE BEST *DEN MOTHER* EVER.
CITY, STOP IT. JUST SMOKE THE DAMN THING SO WE CAN GO BY THE FIRE. IT'S COLD.
YEAH, WELL...
...IT'S ALWAYS COLD HERE IN THE DARK.

HOW YOU DOING, MILES?
I'M ALIVE, WHICH IS MORE THAN I SHOULD BE ABLE TO SAY.
LOOKS LIKE LADY LUCK'S GOT A CRUSH ON YOU.
WELL, I *AM* PRETTY.
YOU HEAR? WE'VE GOT THREE PRESIDENTS NOW.
YEAH, AND WE'LL PROBABLY HAVE *TWELVE* MORE TOMORROW. MAYBE EVEN A *KING* OR TWO.
LIKE THE ALIENS AREN'T BAD ENOUGH. HOW THE HELL ARE WE SUPPOSED TO KNOW WHO'S IN CHARGE?
EASY. THEY *ALL* ARE.
OUR CIVILIZATION IS DYING. AND ITS DEATH WON'T BE PRETTY.
YOU'RE HIGH. ALIENS OR NOT, THIS IS STILL AMERICA.
DUKE, WE WERE LYNCHED IN BROAD DAYLIGHT BECAUSE WE TRIED TO HELP A BLACK MAN SAVE HIS DAUGHTER. SHERIFF LIZZY BORDEN WAS RIGHT. AMERICA'S DEAD.
WHAT ABOUT THE REST OF THE WORLD? ENGLAND, CHINA? HELL, CANADA.
I DON'T KNOW, LET'S PUT ON *CNN* AND FIND OUT.
WISE ASS.
LOOK, ALL I'M TRYING TO SAY IS THAT NO ONE IS COMING TO HELP US.
WE'RE ON OUR OWN.
THIS YOUR WAY OF TELLING ME YOU WANT TO BE PRESIDENT?
VERY FUNNY.
BUT *KING* MILES HAS A PRETTY GOOD RING TO IT.
WELL, *YOUR MAJESTY,* YOUR SUBJECTS ARE STARVING AND YOUR ARMY CONSISTS OF A COUPLE OF HANDGUNS AND AN AUTISTIC KID WITH A WOODEN SPOON.
NO OFFENSE, BUT YOUR KINGDOM SUCKS.
HEH HEH. YEAH, I SUPPOSE IT DOES.
BUT IT'S A START.